'That u

The horrific admission hung between them, and he watched its meaning dawn in Paige's eyes. Kieran dropped his hands from the slender, fragile shoulders that did nothing to convey the true strength he knew lay inside Paige's steely will.

What he'd told her—what he was—was more than he could expect her to accept. He'd been the scientist, but he'd become the deadly experiment.

As his wife and a fellow PAX agent, Paige knew enough to know that the activation serum could be dangerous. She had no idea *how* dangerous.

"You were contaminated with the activation," she breathed into the eerie stillness left behind by his words. She reached out, and the shocking tenderness of her fingers touching his face filled him with intolerable longing. Her eyes were huge, dark, liquid. "What's happened to you?"

"You don't want to know."

Dear Reader,

Greetings! This is the first month that Silhouette Intimate Moments switches from six to four books, and we are delighted to bring you a strong selection of page-turning stories. Of course, the best way to beat the heat is to pick up July's adrenaline-rush reads. As you curse your failing air conditioner and wish you could take that exotic trip with [insert handsome action superstar here], relieve the stress by delving into the emotional ride where passengers fall in love during life's most extraordinary circumstances.

USA TODAY bestselling author Beverly Barton delights readers with a new romance from her popular miniseries, THE PROTECTORS. In *Ramirez's Woman* (#1375), a female bodyguard poses as a sexy politician's fiancée in order to foil a perilous threat on the campaign trail. Reader favorite Carla Cassidy returns with another WILD WEST BODYGUARDS story, *Defending the Rancher's Daughter* (#1376), in which a rancher hires her long-ago crush to protect her from harm. Can she keep herself from falling in love again?

Suzanne McMinn will bring out the beast in you with *The Beast Within* (#1377), the first in her PAX miniseries, in which a tantalizing hero shows his primal nature…and his estranged wife is charged with taming him! Harlequin Historical veteran Mary Burton debuts in the line with *In Dark Waters* (#1378), a creepy and provocative story about two divers who share a sizzling attraction as they investigate a grisly murder mystery.

These four stellar authors will fire up your summer and keep you looking for the adventure in your world. Be sure to return for next month's exciting lineup!

Happy reading!

Patience Smith
Associate Senior Editor
Silhouette Intimate Moments

The Beast WITHIN

SUZANNE McMINN

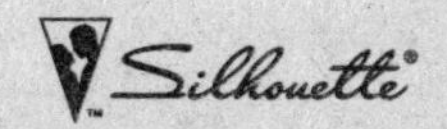

INTIMATE MOMENTS™
Published by Silhouette Books
America's Publisher of Contemporary Romance

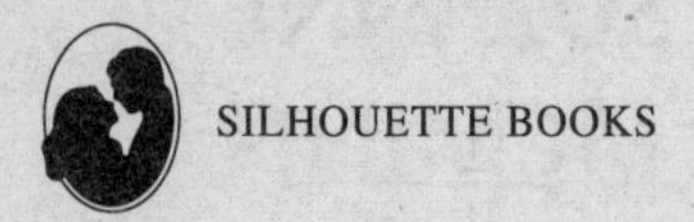

ISBN 0-373-27447-5

THE BEAST WITHIN

This edition published by arrangement with Harlequin Books S.A.

Visit Silhouette Books at www.eHarlequin.com

Printed in U.S.A.

Books by Suzanne McMinn

Silhouette Intimate Moments

Her Man To Remember #1324
Cole Dempsey's Back in Town #1360
**The Beast Within* #1377

Silhouette Romance

Make Room for Mommy #1191
The Bride, the Trucker and the Great Escape #1274
The Billionaire and the Bassinet #1384

*PAX

SUZANNE McMINN

lives by a lake in North Carolina with her husband and three kids, plus a bunch of dogs, cats and ducks. Visit her Web site at www.SuzanneMcMinn.com to learn more about her books, newsletter and contests. Check out www.paxleague.com for news, info and fun bonus features connected to her "PAX" series about paranormal superagents!

With huge thanks to my editor, Shannon Godwin, for being as excited about this series as I was, and with love to my husband for all his support and collaboration.

Prologue

Light blinded him as the lab exploded.

One second, he was performing a routine test procedure with his partner, Phil Bennett, and the next, Kieran Holt's life blew apart. His hands flew up to shield his face as heat pushed at him, whirling past him in a thunderous roar. A mighty crack tore through his consciousness and he rocked backward.

Suddenly it wasn't the fire *outside* his body he felt but *within*—fever, aching, cramps. An extreme stinging and itching took over his body, then gut-wrenching nausea and cell-ripping pain.

He was dying. He had to be dying. And he'd never

see, hold, touch Paige again if he didn't fight. He opened his eyes to find himself on the floor of the lab, slightly below the thick smoke.

Fire was everywhere, chemicals shattering in violent, changing light. He battled through the strange agony engorging his skin, humming pressure through his blood. He had to escape, and he had to find Phil. Every move he made came with slicing pain somewhere inside his body.

His vision cleared and he saw the booted leg sticking out from behind the work table. He crawled toward it and found his partner's empty eyes staring up at him in the eerie, swarming inferno. Grief choked him along with noxious fumes.

Kieran struggled to his feet, but balance was impossible. He felt drunk, drugged, barely capable of walking on two legs. He stumbled back onto all fours as grayish ectoplasmic vapor erupted from his own skin.

Time and space lost all meaning. He knew a shifting, excruciating energy as a warm chill rushed through his body, and he stared in horror as a prickling burst out on his arms and legs. With a ferocious will, he forced himself onto his feet and exploded from the lab. Men—security officers—rushed toward him down the corridor. He stumbled past them, rushing from the building in dazed involuntary instinct. Cool night air struck his face, but the heat within didn't die.

He felt his proportions change—his face stretch, his hips narrow, his shoulders evaporate into his torso. His senses splintered and he could no longer think in words but in emotions and sensations as if his mind had been taken apart and put back together all wrong.

All he knew was panic, and all he could do was run.

Chapter 1

Paige Holt gave an instinctive pat to the inside front pocket of her rain slicker, reassuring herself that the documents were still there. All she needed was one signature, from one man, on one piece of paper.

"Forecasters expect Bernadette to strengthen before making landfall on the barrier islands and eastern seaboard late tonight. More details will be available around eight p.m. when Air Force Reserve hurricane hunters pay Bernadette a return visit—"

She would be long gone by then. Long gone… and free.

The National Hurricane Center broadcast crackled fuzzily in the chartered helicopter. The pilot shifted the controls, taking the craft into its vertical descent. The almost primordial island beach-bound forest of loblolly pines, live oaks and palmetto trees rose up toward her, deceptively quiet. Callula Island.

Was Kieran really here?

They went way back, she and Kieran. Back to their early days at PAX, when she'd actually thought they could do anything as long as they were together. Could she have been more naive? She'd been attracted to him right from the start, with his dark hair a little too long, his hard smile a little too wide, his umber-brown eyes a little too dangerous.

She'd loved the way he watched her, steady and confident and full of some breathtaking energy that had zeroed in on her from the very start. He'd had a way of making her feel special, as if he couldn't see anyone but her. And that sense of overwhelming rightness had sucked her needy heart into a soul a little too damaged, a spirit a little too dark. She'd thought she could heal him, that all it took was love.

Naive didn't begin to cut it.

She missed him and hated him and panic welled up inside her at the thought of seeing him again.

The light single-engine helicopter she'd chartered to take her to the drumstick-shaped barrier island bumped down on the wide strip of sand. Her stomach danced and a lump moved into her throat.

"This is it, ma'am," the pilot said over the dying noise of the rotary motors as he killed the engine. "Callula Island. You've got till six p.m., latest. Then I'm out of here."

He gave her a look that told her he already thought this trip was crazy. She'd paid the Savannah-based charter pilot double to fly her here in the face of an approaching hurricane. No one in their right mind would take off with this kind of weather coming, he'd suggested.

Since when had she been in her right mind?

"You can't pay me enough to stay past six," he added for good measure, just in case she was considering that added foolishness.

"I'll be back by six."

Calulla Island was four miles long, two miles wide. Paige was in shape, and dressed for hiking. They'd made an exploratory flyover that put the majority of Callula out of the question for a hiding place.

The island was a mix of natural communities—from marshland to forest within a surprisingly short geographic area. The marshes and dunes of the lower portion of the island made it easy to dismiss. The northern end, with its maritime jungle, was the part she would have to hike into on foot.

She had six hours to find a man who didn't want to be found.

The pilot got out, and Paige pushed open the passenger door of the helicopter. She jumped out, walked around the side. Sand crunched beneath her boots. The late May air felt cool on her face. A light breeze, in no way suggestive of the storm to come, fingered through the blonde hair she'd left hanging loose to her shoulders.

She felt Kieran's spirit as she gazed into those dark, thick woods. He was here.

He *had* to be here.

She came around the side of the helicopter. Shells littered the beach. Far across the water, a dolphin broke the still-calm surface. Dolphins meant luck, and she needed some today.

She found the pilot leaning up against the rear cargo door, his ropey build taut as he gazed out at the ocean. He flicked his Bic, lit a cigarette. He leaned his head back as he sucked in, his dark hair teasing the collar of his denim-blue shirt. His hawkish, sharp eyes watched her as he blew out.

Paige hadn't smoked in five years, but she almost begged him for a hit.

Dammit, she wasn't going to feel anything. Not anxiety. Not regret. Not grief. Nothing. She was so good at lying to herself, it was almost scary.

She turned her back on the pilot, the helicopter, and any half-baked notion of going home. She'd spent months trying to find Kieran. Now she was here.

And she was damn well going to get what she came for.

Kieran didn't care about her. Maybe he never had, despite their three years of marriage. He'd abandoned her and the PAX League without the slightest effort at defending himself or explaining the mystery of that final, fatal night.

How could he have so completely turned his back on everything they believed in? How could he have turned his back on her?

She'd seen the evidence, and it had damned him. Even so, the charges against him had been hard to buy. But she'd had to buy one thing—he'd left her, without a word of explanation or even a goodbye.

Now, she just wanted the long nightmare to end. She wanted a new life, and that meant leaving PAX.

And divorcing Kieran.

She left the beach and entered the thick woods. A rush of birds lifted up from the trees, the beat of their wings filling the air above her, followed by a scampering—squirrels, or raccoons—from somewhere ahead. Through the shadows, she heard the tap-tap of a woodpecker. The maritime forest was home to countless animals, including the red wolf that Kieran had spent so much time studying as part of his work in PAX.

She supposed it wasn't so strange that when he'd taken flight, he had buried himself in a place that was home to those same wolves.

She'd written, called, finally visited every family member, colleague, friend, distant acquaintance of Kieran's. PAX had looked for him, too, she knew. He was their agent, even if he had turned his back on them. They wanted him back—and not to continue his ectoplasmic research. When they found him, he would be placed in a prison isolation facility for the rest of his life if what they believed about him was true.

For some stupid reason she didn't dare examine, she couldn't stand the thought of Kieran living the rest of his life in a government lockup. And maybe she was as crazy as they believed he was to still believe he could be innocent of the terrible charges that had been lodged against him. She'd conducted her own search quietly, carefully, behind the scenes.

When she'd visited Kieran's cousin, Dub Walker, for the third time and he'd finally admitted he knew where she could find him...*if* she promised to keep Kieran's secret, she'd agreed. And Dub had believed her for one reason.

She had loved Kieran with all her heart.

But like the song said, what did love have to do with it? Love had betrayed her, broken her soul, destroyed her dreams. She'd trusted him. And he'd let her down in the worst way.

She wasn't sure what she wanted now, but she knew it had to start with closure. She could have divorced Kieran without the signature—there were ways, she'd investigated them. But she'd never be able to move on without facing him, one last time.

Damn Kieran for making it so hard.

She kept an eye on the time as she worked her way into the island forest. It was a strange, almost post-apocalyptic atmosphere of slash pine growth born of the disruptive force of fires and hurricanes that occasionally recreated the barrier island habitat. Shade-tolerant hardwood reached up within the pines, slowly taking over the swampy wood with hauntingly romantic palmettos and live oaks strung with creeper vines and Spanish moss.

The maritime jungle was so thick, the canopy of leaves cloaked the sky, and it was preternaturally shadowed, a world of endless twilight and unknowable sounds. Paige carefully hiked a grid pattern through the woods, mindful of the approaching weather...and the eerie sensation of being watched.

The noise of the helicopter must surely have announced her arrival. He would know it wasn't Dub. His cousin—at least in his legal line of work—was a commercial fisherman, which was how Kieran had made his way to Callula Island. Dub hadn't given her too many details, but she knew Dub brought Kieran supplies on a regular basis. Not directly to the island, but in sealed bundles packed in crates and set free such that they would eventually come ashore on Callula's long beach. Every precaution had been taken along the way to protect the secrecy of Kieran's location.

"He could be dead for all I know," Dub had told her. "How could he have survived all this time, alone, on that island? But the crates keep disappearing off the beach. And so I keep bringing them. I don't want to believe he's dead."

Paige understood how he felt. She didn't want to believe Kieran was dead either. He had been the most vibrant person she'd ever known.

And she would know if he had died, wouldn't she?

He was alive. She felt him watching her. Her pulse sped, and she glanced back, almost expecting to see him there. Eyes glowed out at her from the dense brush of the thick woods.

Kieran.

Then the eyes moved, and a shape formed from the shadows. It was a wolf, sleek and lean and beautiful. Paige watched the creature for a long moment, a sense of loss keening through her chest as it disappeared back into the forest.

She was too close to the edge, emotionally, and she had to get hold of herself. She was imagining things. Imagining Kieran's eyes on her. Imagining that she knew Kieran, could feel Kieran.

How utterly, painfully ridiculous.

What if he was dead? What if she found his body, his skeleton?

She felt sick, and with all the training PAX had given her, she blanked the image of Kieran, dead, from her mind. She looked at her watch, pushed the button that lit the digital display. She'd been searching for three hours. Her legs hurt and her lungs burned as she kept up a steady pace. She had no time to waste. She had to keep on track, keep moving.

Had Dub lied to her? She couldn't dismiss the possibility, but she had to search, had to hope that he'd told her the truth.

Continuing to hike the grid she'd mapped out, she found herself on higher ground. The forest became less swampy, more rocky and hilly, though still dense. Above, wind rustled louder.

The storm was coming. The helicopter pilot would be impatient. The hurricane was real, and it was coming, and she couldn't ignore its dangers.

Suddenly, from out of the forest, a cliff-face rose before her. It took long, thudding pulse beats for her to recognize the large yawning darkness near the bottom for what it was—a cave. It blended into the mossy rock so seamlessly, she'd almost missed it.

She barely felt her feet, barely breathed, as she took one step, then another, as if in slow motion. She felt every pound of her heart. Blood rushed in her ears.

Then a hand clamped down on her mouth, an arm took hold of her waist, and an achingly familiar voice ground in her ear, "I want you off my island *now.*"

* * *

He twisted her in his arms, forcing her to face him. Paige's eyes were wide, frightened—of him—and a gasp of shock exploded out of her against his palm. He knew what she saw, and it wasn't the Kieran Holt she'd known. His brown hair was long, to his shoulders, and he hadn't shaved in months. He was as wild as anything on this godforsaken island. Wilder.

And much more dangerous.

"Don't scream," he warned her, still holding tightly to her arms even as he dropped his hand from her mouth. She had adrenaline charging her strength, but he was stronger. Especially these days.

She blinked, said nothing, just stared at him for a long, horrible beat. He could feel her body trembling against him, feel her soft warmth even in the thick chill of the approaching storm.

"Kieran," she breathed finally, almost a question, as if she couldn't believe her eyes.

She smelled like lemons and sunrises and faraway dreams. It was nearly drugging, holding her this way. His sense of smell, like his eyesight, was sharper now. Almost painfully so. And nothing was more painful in his dark world than Paige.

He couldn't bear to look in her eyes, that damnably burning blue that he could still see all too well, and found himself looking everywhere else—at her sweet, wide mouth, pale golden hair feathering across her smooth cheeks, chest rising in fast breaths. Her body felt tense.

It had been too long since he'd held Paige. The ruined heart he might as well not have anymore thundered in his chest. Fiery grief stung his heart, all the worse for having been so deliberately, carefully, suppressed for so long.

She wasn't supposed to be here. She didn't belong here, could never belong here. Her presence went against every plan, every strategy, every hope in hell he had of ever getting off this island.

And he did mean hell. Callula Island was his own personal level of Dante's *Inferno*, a never-ending nightmare that had begun the night his laboratory had exploded around him.

He focused on the things hc had to know, thc answers he'd needed from the moment he'd heard the helicopter flying over Callula. Since Paige had landed, he'd stalked her, soundlessly, through the woods.

"How did you know I was on this island?"

"Dub." The admission was low, hoarse. She struggled against him. Her frame was slight, her limbs slender, but she was stronger than she looked.

He met her eyes, and as he'd known they would, her eyes stabbed him, hated him. He knew what she must think. She would think he'd betrayed PAX. She'd believe he and Phil had planned to steal their own research, sell it—the activation serum they'd spent years developing along with the containment serum. She'd believe he'd set fire to the lab—a fire in which Phil had ultimately died—to cover up the crime. A fire in which, ironically, their research, their work, and *both* the serums had been destroyed. She'd believe all of that and more, and she had to keep believing because it kept her safe. But that didn't make it any easier for him.

Those secrets, those truths, couldn't be revealed to her. His innocence was an empty badge of honor.

"Who else knows I'm here?" he asked.

How long had he thought this harbor would last? He was grateful Dub had held out this long. His cousin had always lived on the shady side of the law, and keeping Kieran's secrets from government agencies wouldn't have been a stretch for him. He had no doubt PAX would have questioned Dub relentlessly, but Dub hadn't broken. His cousin hadn't known the exact reason Kieran was hiding out, but Dub would never turn him in to the authorities. But he'd told Paige, and that was in many ways worse.

"No one," she said. "Just me." She struggled in his hands again, kicked at him, hit his leg with the toe of her boot. A slash of pain, meaningless in his world of pain, seared his calf. "Let go of me, Kieran."

"You have no idea how much I want to do just

that," he growled. Every second that he faced her killed him a little bit more.

Her devastatingly blue eyes were nothing like he remembered. Her soul was in her eyes, that's what he'd always said about Paige. But now her eyes were hard, protected. She'd changed, and he knew he was to blame. Her life had never been easy, and he'd made it a hell of a lot harder. Guilt, ever near the surface, twisted its knife.

"What about the helicopter pilot?" he demanded, fierce because he couldn't allow himself to be otherwise. For her sake, she had to keep hating him.

"He doesn't know why I came here," she said, her voice low and angry.

Good. He wanted her angry.

"He didn't ask?"

"I paid him double his normal fee. That was the end of our conversation."

"He knows you're here. That's bad enough."

"I'm not here to cause trouble," she told him, her body still humming with tension

"That you're here at all is trouble," he ground back. More trouble than she could imagine. "Swear to me no one else knows you're here, Paige."

"No one knows. I told you. Dub wouldn't have told me except—" She broke off, looked away for a horrible beat in which Kieran felt as if his chest was being crushed and he didn't even know why, then she said, "I want a divorce, Kieran."

He let go of her. She nearly stumbled backward, as if she hadn't expected it in that instant. He barely held his own ground. Of course. Why hadn't he foreseen it? How had he managed to so block out every agonizing thought of the wife he'd so loved that he hadn't realized one day she would want a divorce? That she would want to move on, make a new life without him?

Was she in love with another man? He almost choked, stopping himself from blurting out the too-revealing question. He couldn't bear the answer, and in truth, that was why he hadn't let himself consider the question in these long two years. He couldn't afford to think of Paige and her life without him.

As if in some kind of surreal dream, he watched her reach inside her rain slicker and pull out a folded pack of papers. And a pen. Paige was always prepared. He almost laughed in bitterness then he saw the brittle shield of her blue eyes slip, saw beyond the steely shield of anger and hatred.

Pain.

Behind the anger, she was hurting, as he was. He would have given anything to tell her the truth—except her life, which was what it could cost.

"If I sign that paper, they'll know you found me," he said harshly, as if he cared more about himself than her. That's what she had to keep thinking. Kieran just knew he didn't want to sign that paper.

"You mean PAX. I'm leaving PAX. They don't know or care what I do anymore."

He didn't ask why she was leaving PAX. He didn't have to. Paige was a passionate spirit. She did things full throttle—or not at all.

He had broken that passionate spirit, at least when it came to PAX. He had disillusioned her the night he'd thrown away her trust.

She'd been so bright and full of hope the day he'd met her early in their training for covert operations. They'd both been recruited into the PAX League's secret under-layer that simmered just beneath its public façade, and if anything, she'd been more eager than he for the wonders it offered her brilliant mind.

The world knew the PAX League as a private foundation dedicated to the philosophical pursuit of global peace. They engaged in human rights missions, environmental campaigns, and charitable projects. And while all those public endeavors were true and beneficial, it wasn't all PAX did.

To over two-thirds of the employees in the PAX League as well as the world, PAX meant *peace* in Latin and stood for nothing further than the organization's devotion to that cause across the globe. But in truth, PAX was an acronym for Paranormal Allied eXperts. Deep in the heart of PAX's Washington,

D.C., building lay a beehive of secret laboratories and experimental studies dedicated to research into the mystical, telepathic, transformational sciences that was leading the world into a new era of defense. *Peace through PAX.*

As a secret PAX agent, Paige had carried on what had begun as a marine engineering project into research in remote underwater communication while Kieran had become part of a mission to develop superpowers of vision, hearing, and strength through combining wolf and human ectoplasm.

Then his laboratory had exploded along with his life. He'd woken to find himself not only a fugitive...but a monster.

And if he didn't get rid of Paige, and soon, she'd find out, too.

"You know that the agency knows everything. Hell, Paige, they probably already know you're here. You're a link to me."

"Then sign the paper."

She made a twisted logic. She was right, it didn't matter. Nothing mattered. He'd had some insane idea that he could fix everything, if he just had enough time. But that wasn't true. He couldn't fix everything.

He couldn't fix what he'd done to Paige.

All he could do was sign her damn paper and hope by some miracle of miracles that PAX would never know Paige had been here. She hadn't come here for his signature, he realized suddenly. She didn't need his John Hancock to get a divorce.

She wanted some kind of agonizing closure. He could give her that, if nothing else.

Then he'd leave Callula. Find another island. Another level of Dante's *Inferno.* He would either find the answer he was looking for, and soon, or the thing inside him would destroy him. He almost didn't care which anymore.

But he could still save Paige.

"Give me the paper." He all but ripped it out of her hands. Without intending to, his fingers brushed hers. Fire flashed through his veins and it took a strength of will honed by two years of loneliness to slowly move away as if he hadn't noticed.

He didn't bother to read the documents. He signed his name and pushed it back at her. "Take it. And go home. Don't come back. Ever." He wanted her out of here, before she found out more. Before he hurt her more than he already had.

She folded the papers back into her rain slicker, tucked the pen in her back pocket. Then she looked up at him with her shining blue eyes.

"Kieran—"

Her voice, heartbreakingly soft now, trailed off. The anger was suddenly gone from her eyes, replaced by concern. Concern for him.

"It's been two years," she went on. "They looked

for you, but—" She shook her head. "Phil was dead. You were gone. Brian quit the agency. PAX closed the project. It's over for everyone…but you."

She didn't understand that it would never be over for him. And just hearing her talk about the past, about people he'd cared about, made it all worse. His partner, Phil Bennett, was dead. Brian Kaplin, his assistant, had left PAX—probably disillusioned, too. And now Paige was leaving the League.

Every person connected to him had been destroyed in one way or another.

"You have what you wanted, Paige. Go. You don't belong here." He couldn't bear her pity. He turned away from her damning eyes.

She said nothing for an interminable beat. He prayed she would walk away.

"You don't belong here, either, Kieran."

He might not have even heard her whispered words if not for the sharpness of his too-keen hearing. He didn't want to hear them.

But she went on.

"You shouldn't have run away from PAX. You should have stayed and faced their questions. You broke your word, turned your back on your duty, on—"

Her. He'd turned his back on her.

"And for what?" she said, louder now, her voice rising against the sound of wind tearing through the pines and palmettos.

The sky was darker. The storm was coming.

"Paige—" He didn't want to turn back, to look at her again. He didn't want to feel, and he couldn't look at her without feeling.

"What are you doing here, Kieran? Living alone—on this deserted island. Like an animal—"

He wheeled on her.

"I *am* an animal, Paige." His voice came out in a snarl, and her eyes grew large. She took a step back from him, but he didn't let her get away. He was scaring her, but he had no choice. He had to make her understand one thing. *She had to leave.*

He gripped her arms again, shook her lightly. "Go away. I don't want to hurt you."

Her gaze was suddenly overbright. "Too late."

He deserved all of the stabbing accusation in her eyes and he knew it. Years shuffled through the foster care system had left its mark on her just as his own biological but miserable home life had left marks, too. Then he'd done the worst thing he could do to someone who'd grown up as she had. He'd abandoned her.

Another long moment passed. Wind howled.

"Paige—" He didn't know what he'd meant to say. There wasn't time to finish. He had let his feelings for Paige distract him, consume all his senses.

It had been a terrible mistake.

A shot cracked past his ear. He thought at first it was a tree snapping in the storm. Then Paige crumpled in his arms.

Chapter 2

The world as she knew it shifted, changed. Pain seared her temple, sudden and nearly blinding. The ground on which she stood swayed, seemed to open a chasm into which she dropped—yet it was no chasm that enclosed her but rather Kieran's arms. Paige was hit by confusing sensations of safety, rightness, fear—but the pain made it all impossible to sort.

She could only stare up at him, locked in by his fierce, protective, angry eyes. Those eyes held her, kept her from the fast-swirling darkness.

The gathering storm over the barrier island receded until there was nothing but Kieran's arms, Kieran's eyes, Kieran's heat.

Then he was gone, somehow, in the time it took her to blink. He'd lowered her to the ground—she knew that. She could feel the soft-packed forest floor beneath her cheek, smell the dirt and the moss. Now a shadow blurred past her eyes.

Low, lithe, dark.

The form streamed across the earth like a ghost, only it was real, she was sure of it. She watched it bound, lifting through the air toward another blurry shadow—a man. There was another sharp explosion, and she realized he was shooting, only comprehending then that she must have been shot. Her gaze spun around wildly, desperate for some point of connection.

Where was Kieran?

The world wavered, and she felt lost. Bright bursts of light crackled before her eyes. She knew she was going to lose consciousness, and she made a desperate attempt to stave off the enfolding blackness, blinking hard, clearing her vision with an effort. The dreamlike quality of the scene gripped her in fear.

The bounding creature reached the man, snarling in lethal fury, and she knew it for what it was. *A wolf.* Faster, more powerful, larger than any wolf she'd ever seen.

The man stumbled backward, screamed. The wolf

latched on to his throat, and they were both down, in a struggle for life or death.

Paige jerked up from the ground, her mind crying Kieran's name, but pain streaked immediately through her head and she couldn't make her lips form the word. The world around her tilted, turned black.

The image waved into her consciousness, blurry, shifting, rippling like water. It was the wolf, red now. Dripping blood. She kept staring, baffled and scared, slowly understanding what she saw.

It wasn't blood. It was some kind of dye. Ochre. She'd seen art like this before, in museums and books. Feather drawn, crude yet sophisticated at the same time. This was not the wolf she'd seen bounding in the shadows of the stormy forest. *That* wolf had been real. *This* was another wolf, created by some primitive hand, springing against a stone backdrop, wild and beautiful. Running free. Hard as the immutable surface on which it was painted and gentle as the soft, blowing breeze that seemed to sweep back its fur.

The wolf pulled at her heart in some inescapable way that baffled her even as it held her fast in its lonely, lost world.

Paige stared at the figure illustrated on the rock surface above her head, her eyes adjusting to the low light, the source somewhere beyond her view, her mind coming awake in dreamy increments. Finally, she tore her gaze from the rock with a sharp force.

Where was she?

She moved, started to push up on her arms, but pain dropped her back down onto something soft, padded. Oh God, her head throbbed. Her whole body ached. And then she remembered—

"Kieran?" she whispered, her voice coming out raw, hoarse.

"Don't move." He appeared above her, and she realized he must have been there all along, at her side. But for how long?

"Where am I?"

"Callula Island."

"No, I mean—" Callula Island. Kieran's home now. His cave. She struggled to put together the pieces from her memory. "The hurricane—"

"You'll have to stay here till it passes." He was doing something, his shockingly tender fingers moving over her head. His nearness was as strange as it was achingly familiar.

"How long was I unconscious?"

He glanced at the watch on his wrist. The leather strap was worn, the clockface scratched. His arm looked like one solid muscle.

"It's about seven o'clock now," he told her. "Several hours."

He was removing some kind of gauze compress

from her forehead, she realized. She felt the rush of air meet her wound, the sting of the raw pain. Still stunned, she took in her surroundings. She was on some kind of pallet, a thin blanket pulled up around her, in an alcove of sorts. Above her, there were those haunting, painted images of wolves running, leaping, flying. Alive in the stone, real inside a dream.

Had Kieran painted them? She had never known him to paint, but she didn't know this Kieran of Callula Island, did she?

Her gaze shifted from the artwork to his face, his expression intent, his powerful hands steady. His touch soothed her and terrified her all at once. It was bizarre, intimate and yet distant. She was closer to him than she'd been in two years, and yet she knew nothing about him—just that the sensation of his touch on her skin brought a fearsome grief that pinched her heart, and she couldn't bear the knowledge of loss that came with it.

She turned her head away slightly, and from the corner of her eye she was drawn to the low glow that seemed to fill a cavernous space, much larger than where she rested now. A vast space filled with the most unlikely of items, utterly incongruous in their otherwise primal, sepulchral environment.

Laboratory equipment. Microscopes, a generator,

a small refrigeration unit, slides, burners, a laptop computer, work lights—

Ointment stung her wound as he dabbed something onto her skin, and she gasped.

"Don't move," he said, his voice grim. "I'm going to put a fresh bandage on the wound. It's just a flesh wound—thank God." He turned away to pick up a fresh bandage that he must have prepared in advance. "I'll get you out of here as soon as possible."

Out of here. Off Callula.

Her mind clicked onto another link and she looked back at Kieran, a hum of understanding beating its way through her pulse. Seven o'clock. Well past the time she was to make the return flight.

"The helicopter pilot—" Panic seized her. He would have left her by now— He'd made it perfectly clear he wouldn't wait.

Kieran's gaze darkened. "Tell me his name. What do you know about him?"

She struggled to put the words together, to remember. "Matt Dinsmore." She felt cold suddenly though the air in the cave was warm, heavy. "He's a charter pilot out of Savannah. Fifteen years experience. Ex-military. I ran a background check myself." She had taken the extra precautions to ensure the secrecy of her trip to Callula. "I have to get off the island."

"The helicopter's still here."

He taped the new bandage with quick, sure movements of his strong fingers. His voice frightened her, it was filled with such ferocity.

"What do you mean, the helicopter's still here? What about the pilot?"

"He's dead."

Paige's pulse thumped. "Dead?"

"He would have killed us both if he'd had the chance." Kieran's face was hard. "I made sure he didn't get the chance."

The shadow of the man with the gun came back to her. The helicopter pilot was the man who had shot her in the woods. Why wasn't even a question yet. She was too shocked. Her mind reeled.

"There was a wolf. It attacked the pilot." Her memory stretched, searched. Where had Kieran been? Why had he left her alone? "You've trained some wolves to protect you?"

He was silent for a long beat, and she was suddenly more scared than she'd ever been in her life. She pushed up to a sitting position. Pain rocked her temples, but she fought through it. The alcove in which she had lain on the pallet was small, low, the painted ceiling of rock just feet above her head. It made her think of a bunk on a ship. Beyond, in its stark, unnatural light, lay the main part of the cave.

No, not a cave, despite its natural setting. A laboratory.

Kieran's laboratory. She looked again at Kieran.

His deep, secret eyes blazed back at her with some unknown pain that went past anything she could have imagined. Questions tangled in her mind. Answers twisted within those questions, answers she didn't want to believe.

"What's going on?" she whispered.

"Lie down, Paige."

She ignored him. "Kieran—"

"I did everything in my power to protect you, Paige." His voice lowered, and a new quality crept into it. Something burned-out, hollow. She didn't know what he was talking about, but she knew it wasn't just about the helicopter pilot. It was something more.

Dread seeped into her from out of nowhere. She watched as he rubbed a frustrated hand over his forehead, and she realized within her own shock that Kieran was exhausted. He looked drawn, pale, as if he'd suffered through some kind of horrific ordeal.

He rose, stretching to his full height as he stepped back from the alcove, back from her. He looked larger than life, like some transcendent being.

"Protect me from what?" she demanded shakily, determinedly pushing past the fear. "What are you doing here, Kieran?"

Sudden comprehension exploded in her mind. Kieran had been developing a way to imbue a PAX agent with extrasensory powers of scent, sight, hearing. The attributes of a wolf. It was what PAX did best—research and create superhuman qualities that enabled their agents to fight terrorism on a level heretofore impossible. Kieran and his partner, Phil Bennett, had been working on a containment serum to control the effects of the activation they'd already perfected. None of the testing had been completed, but its possibilities had ripped through PAX like an electric shock in those days. Everyone had known of the startling potential of the research. Even the Pentagon had been aware—and wary. The impact on the human mind of such transformation held the dormant capacity for unrestrained violence, powers beyond any control. There had been quiet rumbles that the research funding would be pulled, and the PAX chief had fought relentlessly for the project's survival.

Then the lab had blown up, and deadly documents found in Phil's home had told the tale to PAX investigators. He and Kieran had been planning to sell the serums to a terrorist network. Together he and Phil had plotted to cover up the crime by destroying their lab, but something had gone wrong. The activation serum had been destroyed in the fire, along with all the data on the lab computers. Phil had died, and in the panic of his escape, Kieran was believed to have left the now-useless containment serum behind.

With PAX hot on his heels, Kieran had disappeared—without either of the precious serums. PAX wanted Kieran back. They wanted justice.

And Paige wanted answers. How could the gifted, dedicated man she'd wed betray PAX that way? She wanted him to tell her it was all a mistake, that he'd never been involved in the plot with Phil. Even the discovery of the containment serum in their apartment hadn't taken away her questions. Her heart had held on to impossible possibilities.

Knowing his past as she did, she'd understood his flight on some psychological level. Kieran had lived in frightening neighborhoods where he'd slept under his bed instead of on top of it for fear of drive-by shootings. He'd been twelve when his strung-out father had driven their car off a washed-out bridge. Of course his dad had survived while Kieran had nearly drowned himself trying to hang on to his twin sister. When rescue workers arrived, his dad was passed out on the riverbank and Annelie was dead. By the time he was fifteen, his addict father had him doing the driving, and when a drug buy ended in a murder, he'd put the gun in Kieran's hand. Kieran had spent the next three years of his teenage life locked up in a juvenile detention center for a crime he'd never committed.

He'd achieved things no one would ever have expected from the troubled teenage boy he'd been. But there was no way he could let himself be locked up again, for another crime he hadn't committed. She couldn't blame him for not believing in the justice system or even PAX. His life hadn't given him a whole hell of a lot of reason to believe in anything. But that he hadn't believed in *her*— That was what she couldn't forgive.

And now, she had to wonder if she'd been wrong and naive all along to hold on to even a measure of her faith in *him*.

What was he doing? Had the activation serum really burned up? Had Kieran stolen it? Was he recreating the containment serum now? Without it, the activation serum was far too dangerous to utilize. Or was he working to reproduce both serums?

Why else would he be hiding here, reproducing his work, if not to sell it? Everything she'd never wanted to believe ripped into her heart like a knife. Betrayal seared her all over again.

"You're recreating the serums," she whispered starkly, and she wanted him to deny it. She wanted to beg him to give her some rational explanation for everything. Oh, God, if this was true, she'd have no choice. She'd have to do anything in her power to stop him. "I can't let you do this," she said, gazing at him in growing horror. "You're going to have to kill me. Because if you don't, I'm going to turn you in."

"Paige—"

"I just thought you were hiding here on this island

so you didn't have to go to prison. I never wanted to think— How stupid could I be? Was the activation serum really destroyed, or did you just make it appear that way? You decided to sell your own research, and leaving part of it behind only meant it would take you that much longer because you would have to recreate it from scratch."

Kieran spun on her.

"What do you mean, left behind?" he demanded.

"The containment serum was found in our apartment, in your lockbox. They searched everything—"

"What? Where is it? Where is the containment serum now?"

"Why? So you can steal it—again?"

"I thought it was gone. I thought it was destroyed in the fire. I thought there was no hope—"

He turned away again, made a sound in his throat, a keening groan of horror. Then he swung back, eyes so dead she nearly screamed.

"I never tried to sell it, Paige. I never tried to sell any of it. I was framed."

"If that was true, why didn't you stay? Why are you here, with this secret lab?"

The weight of the betrayal in the evidence before her was crushing her. Her heart was dying, right here, right now.

"Tell me where the containment serum is." He came back, took a strong hold of her shoulders as he sat beside her. "If you ever believed me, Paige, believe me now. If you ever loved me, trust this one thing. I have to have it."

Suddenly she was overwhelmed by a terrible foreboding. The force behind his voice terrified her. She didn't want to be humiliated, betrayed, destroyed by him again, but she had no choice about asking the next question.

"Why?"

A nightmarish beat passed in the heavy silence of the cave. The storm outside might as well have been a thousand miles away. In Kieran's laboratory, it was utterly, eerily still.

He finally spoke.

"That was not a trained wolf."

Chapter 3

The horrific admission hung between them and he watched its meaning dawn in Paige's eyes. Kieran dropped his hands from the slender, fragile shoulders that did nothing to convey the true strength he knew lay inside Paige's steely will. What he'd told her—what he was—was more than he could expect her to accept. He'd been the scientist, but he'd become the deadly experiment. Paige knew enough as his wife and a fellow PAX agent to know that the activation serum alone could be dangerous. She had no idea *how* dangerous.

He lived with that horror every day. He might live

with it for the rest of his life—however long that would be. And he didn't expect it to be very long at all now.

"You were contaminated with the activation serum," she breathed into the eerie stillness left behind by his words. "Oh, God." She reached out and the shocking tenderness of her fingers touching his face filled him with intolerable longing. Her eyes were huge, dark, liquid. "What's happened to you?"

The horror in her night-tide depths mixed with grief, and he had to shift back, away from her, in order to keep his head straight. The searing emotion of her eyes and her touch stunned him as much as the information that the original containment serum still existed. And that it had been found in their apartment, in his own lockbox. What did that mean?

His whole world had rocked off its axis and he needed time to think. Abject horror tightened around him, grew exponentially at the possibilities. Worst of all was that now Paige was involved.

He'd already told her more than he'd intended, more than was safe—for her. But he'd had no choice. She'd seen his laboratory. He'd had to stop her from turning him in. And now—

"You don't want to know," he said grimly. "You don't need to know." He had to protect her from the full implications of the information she'd brought to him. She didn't realize the meaning and he didn't want her to realize it. If she did, it would only make things worse for her—-and for him. "What you need to do is to get off this island and forget you ever saw me. Forget you ever *knew* me."

"No," she said immediately. "I can't do that. You're my—" Husband. He was her husband. She broke off, her face etched in pain.

"Whatever we once were to each other, it's over now," he said with bitter force, a force intended to protect her even as the flinch his harsh words brought to her soulful gaze killed him. He didn't want to hurt her, had never wanted to hurt her. She'd come to Callula Island for closure, and he had to give her that. There was no going back to what they'd once had and he had to make sure she understood that.

He was a different man, forever changed, and possibly doomed. Paige deserved more. He'd learned on this island to shut off his emotions, and he had to rely on that skill now.

"As soon as possible, you're getting off this island," he repeated.

"What about you?" she demanded, and he could see the fighting spirit in her unquenched in spite of his brutally cold words. Resilience grew in her eyes. Her chin was high, her shoulders square. "If this is true, you have to go back to PAX. You have to get the serum, and you have to tell them the truth."

"They bought the frame, Paige," he said bitterly. "Who would believe me now, after I ran away?"

When he'd finally come to himself again after the explosion, he'd found himself deep in Rock Creek Park. He'd made it back to his and Paige's apartment building. She'd been asleep and he'd been terrified—of himself. The phone had rung, and he'd overheard that awful conversation she'd had with PAX chief Vinn Regan. And he'd known there was no going back to PAX and that the best thing he could do for Paige was disappear.

He'd waited, hiding, until she'd gone into the bathroom. He'd heard her sobbing over the rain of the shower, and he'd wished he were already dead. He'd slipped out, run across the street, and watched as PAX agents had entered the building moments later. And then he had, quite simply, vanished.

"I knew that day that I wasn't the same man, and might never be again. Without the containment serum, I'm a monster." And he'd known then that PAX believed he was a traitor. He couldn't put Paige through the truth that he was something much worse. He didn't know what he was capable of doing when he shifted. He didn't know if he could hurt Paige. He was a man in fear of himself, and it was why, above all, he'd isolated himself on Callula Island. Its remoteness protected not only him, but protected others from him.

The containment serum hadn't been thoroughly tested. The research hadn't been completed. The intent had been to create a strong enough serum to deactivate the power, should that be required, as well as controlling it through smaller control doses. But there were, in fact, no guarantees the serum would act on him at all after all this time—even if he did get his hands on it.

The end was coming, and much faster than he'd even expected.

Just in the past few weeks, he'd completely lost the cone photoreceptors in his eyes that gave humans full color vision. One step at a time, he was changing, forever. The human inside him was dying, and he had no idea what that meant to his very existence.

As a scientist, he was fascinated. As a man, he was frightened. All he knew for sure was that the end was near and that it would be terrible. He'd had bouts of pain for months, pain that came on with erratic severity, and the bouts were increasing at an alarming rate.

Would he go to sleep one night and wake a wolf—forever?

He knew he was frightening Paige now, and he had to. He wanted her to run away from Callula Island as soon as possible.

Then he had to figure out what to do next. Burning inside him now was the knowledge that he'd been wrong, that the containment serum *hadn't* been destroyed. All this time he had hidden here, trying to recreate it, and it had still existed.

But how had it ended up in his lockbox?

There was only one answer. Someone had planted it there. And it couldn't have been Phil. Had Phil been set up, too? His mind reeled.

Knowing the serum had been found in his lockbox changed everything. Kieran had gone back to the apartment. He'd taken cash out of that lockbox that terrible dawn before he'd fled..

The containment serum hadn't been there—and Phil had already been dead.

Someone else had been involved, someone who'd gone back to Kieran's apartment and planted the seemingly now-useless containment serum to seal the frame of Kieran. PAX had searched the apartment that morning, right after he'd left it, and they'd found the serum.

There was a traitor in PAX. If Phil had been involved, he hadn't acted alone. And the traitor was still there.

"But you have a chance now," Paige said emphatically. "There *is* hope." She reached out again, took hold of his arm, her eyes huge and pleading. "You need the serum, and the serum is at PAX, locked up in your old office. They let me in to clear out your personal effects. I saw Vinn lock the serum in the cabinet. As far as I know, it's still there. They left your office intact, just as it was, in case they needed anything later for the investigation. The project was shut down, the lab and your office sealed. You have to go back for it!"

He didn't want to talk to her about what he had to do. He didn't want her involved. He had to go back, she was right. It was his best chance to survive now, slim as it might be. But Paige didn't have to go back with him, and it could cost her life if she did.

Just the thought of something happening to Paige twisted up his insides. "This has nothing to do with you, Paige."

Her expression stiffened.

"How dare you tell me this has nothing to do with me?" Her voice grew stronger with every syllable. "Do you think it had nothing to do with me when you disappeared?" Woven into her voice was that profound pain that he knew too well and only wished he could forget.

He forced himself to speak with cold determination. "You came here for a divorce, Paige. I gave it to you. It's finished."

It had to be finished, for her sake. This new information changed everything. He had no choice. It wasn't only his own life at stake. The future of PAX could be at risk, too—and that was the last thing he wanted Paige to know. She'd be better off going on with her plans to leave PAX. Then she'd be out of danger, once and for all.

No way was he doing anything that would put her in the bull's-eye that he now knew was waiting.

"You're going to take your signed papers and go on with your life," he all but growled at her. "That's how I want it." She'd stepped out of his sweet dreams and into his all too deadly nightmare. He needed her back safely in his dreams.

In the shadows of the alcove, his keen sight knew too clearly her defiant eyes. "And what about what I want?" she asked quietly.

"You wanted closure. Here's your closure. It's over. If you wanted more than that, you made a mistake. I don't have more to give you."

He felt the cruelty of his statement in the heat of her hurting gaze. But he couldn't allow what she'd learned about him to lead her to believe anything could change between them.

Then he told the worst lie of all.

"I want this divorce, even if you don't."

He left her, strode away into the open cavern of his laboratory. Paige stared after him, controlling the tears that threatened to spill from her eyes. She blinked rapidly to bring the cave back into focus. She was battling so many emotions, she had no idea where to start in dealing with them.

Shock still hummed through her body. If Kieran had been contaminated with the activation serum—

What had it done to his body, his mind? What was going to happen to him now?

He'd gone two years without the containment serum. That alone was almost unbelievable. And even if he got his hands on the serum now, would it save him?

She'd never understood what had happened that night, and she was only more confused now. She'd yearned for answers for so long, but all she had now were more questions. It had been hard to believe Phil had been a traitor, working with terrorists. Even harder to believe Kieran had been, too.

If he'd been in the apartment that morning— His life depended on that containment serum. He wouldn't have full control of his wolf side without it. He could, as he'd said, end up a monster. He wouldn't have left it behind, not after he'd been contaminated by the activation serum. But it was a fantastical story, one her heart was too eager to latch on to and run with.

And she had good reason not to trust her heart. Or Kieran. He was hiding something from her, of that she was certain.

She followed him, not finished—not by a long shot. Her knees felt rubbery and her head light, but she wasn't letting anything stop her from finding out what he planned to do now.

Kieran turned, and she saw the unforgiving line of

his jaw, the harsh angles of his cheekbones, the brutal intensity of his gaze. But in the glow of the cave, she saw something else in his eyes that shocked her. She'd seen their hollowness, but she realized now they burned with an almost eerie energy. They were familiar and unfamiliar all at the same time. And she understood now where that energy came from.

The containment serum had been intended to control the activation of the wolf powers, integrate fully the exchange of ectoplasm. The activation had never been intended to be taken alone, without its companion control.

He wasn't the same man she'd known. But no way could she turn her back on this new Kieran, even if he didn't love her anymore—because even now, she could see the Kieran she had known deep inside those shocking eyes. She remembered the way his fingers used to feel on her face, the way his mouth felt on her lips, the way her heart would pump whenever he came near. To think of what could happen to him now made something inside her shatter. And if she was kidding herself that she could deal with this horror, she didn't want to know.

"Our marriage may be over," she said, mustering all the strength in her aching, damnably shaking body, "but I'm still a PAX agent. And so are you."

"You're leaving PAX," he said. "And I left PAX a long time ago. And dammit, Paige, you're about to drop. You have no business being on your feet." He reached out and took hold of her just as her weak, rebellious knees began to give out.

His strong arms pulled her up into his hold. She breathed in the male scent of him, her cheek resting against his broad chest. For a surreal moment, she was thrown back in time to the days when being held this way by Kieran was something she'd both loved and taken for granted. The wound of two years without him bled anew.

He deposited her on a crude wooden chair by one of the work tables. The air in the cave was warm and heavy from the generator-powered heater, but when he stepped away, she felt only cold emptiness. Her throat felt thick with feelings she couldn't allow. She had to keep her head clear.

"If you didn't leave that containment serum in the apartment, then someone else did," she said quietly, watching him, working to distance herself from the storming emotion and focus on the question at hand.

Her head hurt and her body felt stupidly weak. She hated weakness, always had—in herself much more than in others. She'd gotten through everything in her life by relying on a determined spirit, and she had to call on that strength now. Her own observation pierced deep, bringing with it an old ache.

He was ignoring her, but she went on: "The terrorists haven't forgotten about you. Maybe when they realized you hadn't died in the lab, too, they thought by making sure you were framed that then you would go to them for help since you couldn't go back to PAX. But you didn't, and now they've found you." She worked to follow the dark path of the plot. "They still want the secrets of the serums—and you're the only one who has them."

Her mind was spinning. She didn't know what made sense anymore. How had they planted the serum in his lockbox in their apartment? But who else would be after him other than terrorists? PAX wanted him back, but if that pilot had been connected to PAX, he would have revealed himself as a PAX agent, demanded Kieran's surrender. If PAX knew about Callula Island, there would be a dozen agents here taking him in.

Kieran turned and walked across the lab, his posture stiff and remote. He reached down and took something out of the refrigeration unit.

"We need PAX's help," she said fiercely. "You did the wrong thing two years ago to run away. Don't make the same mistake now."

Kieran turned and strode back to her. His face was a grim mask, and she knew he was unconvinced by her arguments even before he spoke. His hard face forewarned her of his icy resolve.

"*We* don't need anything," he said with equal fervor to her own. "Drink this." He shoved a can of juice toward her. "I'm not the one you should be worrying about. You could have died today."

And she could have sworn she saw a sheen of emotion in his eyes then, even though he'd made it quite clear he didn't want anything more to do with their marriage. The shadow of a struggle played in those dangerous depths, as if he fought with feelings just as she did. But she couldn't let herself go down that path of thought. That way led to madness. She couldn't bear to hope for a future with Kieran when he'd made it quite clear he saw no future at all—with her or without her.

I want this divorce, even if you don't.

Dammit, she didn't *want* a future with Kieran any more than he wanted one with her. She didn't even know if she could trust him. And that shouldn't have been so hard for her to remember. But every time she looked at him, she felt as if a twenty-foot wave crashed over her head.

"It was my fault the pilot found you," she said starkly, her heart squeezing. "I led him to you."

For that reason alone, she had to convince Kieran to get help. And if she could convince herself that was the only reason she couldn't walk away from him, then she'd be a lot better off.

"It's not your fault, Paige. You're not responsible for me."

His words did nothing to assuage her guilt. She

watched as he turned, reached into the refrigeration unit again, and took out a package of something wrapped in plastic. She realized the work table she was sitting beside was set up like a little camp kitchen. There was a small propane stove, tin dishes, and utensils crammed in an empty coffee can.

She took a sip of the cold drink and watched him as he unwrapped the bundle of what she realized was fish and dumped it in a small pan. He took fresh vegetables from a crate and chopped them into the pan and turned on the burner. He worked efficiently, no wasted motions. The cave loomed around them, contrasting the primitive with the modern.

"Dub brings you all of this," she said. How had Kieran lived like this for two years? The loneliness of the experience struck her.

"He drops off crates when he can. I pick them up off the beach. I catch the fish. He sends me fresh vegetables and fruits. In the beginning, he sent me the equipment and supplies for the lab."

She hadn't been surprised to discover it was Dub helping Kieran. Kieran had told her once that when they were kids and played cops and robbers, Dub had always wanted to be the robber. She'd never known exactly what Dub did when he wasn't fishing, but she'd always been pretty sure it had been some kind of smuggling. Dub wasn't the kind of man who lived by anyone's laws.

But he'd do anything for Kieran, and she'd known that, too. It was the one thing she and Dub had in common, and the one reason Dub had told her about the island.

"Does Dub know why you're here, know what you're doing?" she asked, though she suspected the answer.

"No. He only knows what he needs to know. I don't want Dub in danger."

Kieran's attention remained intent on his task. His dark hair hit shoulders that were as broad as ever, but more muscular in the plain tee he wore that hugged his biceps. His jeans were faded and threadbare in places. He was leaner, more sinewy than before.

And even now, when she was frightened and hurt and still had every reason to hate him, she felt a tremble in her stomach when she looked at him. She had never met a man more dangerously sexy even when he wasn't even trying. And when he tried— Oh God, when he tried, he was off the charts.

The pungent aroma of the fish steamed around her. He stirred the mixture with a large steel spoon.

"When did you start painting the wolves?" she asked. The art fascinated her. There was something in the freedom of the strokes that said something, but she wasn't sure what. He had to despise the darkness within him, and yet he'd honored it in the most beautiful, primitive way.

"It was a way to pass the time," he answered simply.

"Surely it was more than that." She didn't intend to let him off the hook. "You weren't painting palmetto trees or owls. You were painting what was inside you. And the art is beautiful."

"What's inside me isn't beautiful, Paige." His voice was brutal and cold.

Then she understood. He was painting a dream.

He claimed to be a man with no hope, and yet he'd painted the purest expression of hope for himself in those wolves running free, carried by the wind.

And he wouldn't admit that to her. He wouldn't admit he held any hope in his heart for himself, his future. He wouldn't share that with her. And that cut deeper than anything else.

"You've been alone, all this time," she said quietly, forcing her mind off the hopeless need that he would let her in, let her share his pain. "I can't imagine what that was like."

"I had work to do."

"I wish you had let me help you." The words blurted out of her, traitorous. She would have run away with him if he'd wanted her to. She would have done *anything* for him then. It was shamefully, pathetically true. If he'd asked her to go to the moon, she would have packed her bag in ten seconds flat.

He lifted his ominous gaze from the stove. "It was better this way."

"You made that decision for me," she said, and she couldn't help the bitterness that threaded into her voice. She swallowed thickly, beating back the hurt, letting anger surge in its place. "You had no right."

He dumped the meal into a plate and shoved it across the table to her along with a fork. He'd prepared nothing for himself.

"Eat. You're going to need your strength tomorrow." He strode away from her, toward a low tunnel-like fissure in the stone.

"Where are you going?"

"Outside to check on the storm."

He was gone. Restless and furious, she sat there for a long beat staring after him. A smart woman wouldn't heed the ache in her chest, wouldn't yearn to steal the darkness from the man Kieran had become. But she was no longer a smart woman, and all she longed to do was run after him and find some way to help him.

She picked at the food. It was good in a bland sort of way, but she didn't want it. She made herself eat enough to fuel her body, though. Kieran was right about one thing, she did need her strength for tomorrow.

And she still needed answers.

Across the room, the work table with his equipment and supplies drew her through the low light. She pushed back the nearly-emptied plate and walked toward it. The table was organized, chemicals neatly labeled, tools laid out in orderly fashion. She picked up a notebook and realized it was his log. She scanned the data he'd input on the opening pages in the strong, clear handwriting that brought a pang to her chest.

Her head still felt light, her knees like Jell-O. She curled up on the hard floor to read. She flipped through the notebook quickly to see if she could define how far along he was in reproducing the serum, but she didn't know enough about the project to tell. He'd been working since his arrival on the island. She realized he'd used the log as a sort of calendar, keeping track of the dates. Days had turned into months had turned into years.

Something fell out of the book and she picked it up. It was a photograph of her, with Kieran. He had his arm lazily draped over her and they were both smiling. They were on the couch in the living room of their apartment. She remembered the day like it was yesterday—it had been her birthday. Kieran had given her a lapis lazuli necklace. He'd said it reminded him of her eyes. The picture was worn, as if it had been rubbed a thousand times.

Had Kieran looked at this photograph alone in his

cave? Had he remembered her and missed her the way she'd missed him?

The questions were too much in the face of his harsh words still ringing in her mind. She inserted the photograph back into the book and flipped to the beginning again, prepared to pore over every page.

An arm swooped down, tore the book in brutal fashion from her grasp.

"The storm will hit soon," Kieran grated. "Go back to the pallet. Rest."

He knelt, opened a chest beneath the table and stuffed the log inside it. She saw a flash of green paper in the chest. Cash. *And a gun.* He clicked the chest shut before he stood. When she didn't move, he reached for her, pulling her to her feet.

He went on: "You've been injured and the last thing I need is for you to collapse. You need to be ready for whatever it's going to take for me to get you off this island tomorrow."

His words were cool, remote, and that remoteness drove her crazy.

"I want to know what you're planning to do after that," she told him determinedly. "You know that going to PAX is the right thing to do."

He ignored her comment. "If the helicopter isn't destroyed, I should be able to fly you out of here by tomorrow afternoon."

The pilot had landed the craft on the leeward

beach. It would be protected from the main onslaught of the winds by the higher ground of the rest of the island. As part of the secret project that had taken Kieran and Phil to remote areas for wild wolf observation and data gathering, Kieran had been trained to fly in order to limit the number of people required on research expeditions.

He was fully capable of flying her out of here, and he was making it quite clear he couldn't wait. After tomorrow, she might never see him again.

He'd held her by her shoulders, but he let go now. He was dismissing her, but she would not be dismissed. She didn't want to be shut out.

"Then what?"

"I'll leave you some place safe."

"And then?"

"Then I'll do what I have to do. It's none of your concern, Paige." The lines around her mouth hardened. "Stop asking questions."

"Anything but going straight to Vinn is insane," she clipped out.

His frightening, burning eyes didn't flinch. This close, he seemed to loom in front of her, fierce and almost otherworldly. She shivered, and yet she was still unable to accept the finality of his words.

"Do you think I'm a sane man, Paige?" A taut, awful beat passed then he spoke again, his voice low. "Do you think I'm even a man anymore?"

Silence gathered, exposing the beat of her heart, the blood pounding in her ears.

"You want me to be scared of you, but I'm not."

Oh, she was scared, but more of her own rebellious heart than of Kieran. She wanted a divorce, closure, a new beginning. But her yearning, foolish heart wanted other things, too.

He was so achingly close, she couldn't resist the urge to touch him, to prove to her and to him that he was as human as she. His whiskers felt unbelievably soft despite the harsh look of them.

"I'm not going to give up on you, even if you've given up on yourself. You're still a man, Kieran." She touched his chest, put her hand over his heart through his shirt. She could feel his blood pumping in his veins, feel his life force. "And if all of this is true, you need me." And he needed PAX.

His gaze on her was furious.

"I don't need anyone. You shouldn't have come here." He took hold of her shoulders again and his quiet voice turned dark and dangerous. "You should have left well enough alone."

"Well enough?" She was the angry one now. "Do you think I have been *well enough* for the past two years? If you hadn't left me without a word, maybe I wouldn't have had to come here," she charged back at him. "If you want to blame anyone for why I'm here, blame yourself."

And then she regretted her rash words because she saw it in his eyes. He did blame himself. Deep within those searing, impenetrable eyes of his, she saw the guilt and the loneliness and the grief.

She would have torn away from him then, afraid—not of him, but of herself—but he held her fast. Heat surged in her cheeks, and the beat stretched to the breaking point as she waited for him to speak.

"I don't want anything to happen to you," he said harshly. "I can't bear it if—"

"If what?" she cried softly, her voice coming out wispy and thin, and a frantic pulse throbbed inside her. Her body hungered to close the narrow gap between them, to tear away the scab of memory and take what the moment offered even if it brought new scars. In the stark silence of the cave, she knew a rushing sound from far away, outside. The storm was coming.

And in that instant, his mouth crushed hers.

Chapter 4

She tasted like hope and promise and a life he'd lost a long time ago. He felt the warmth of her body, the softness of her breath. She was everything he'd given up and could never have again, and yet he throbbed for her with an unbearable, illogical demand. His hand moved around her to clutch the silken tangle of her hair. She melted in his arms, and that was all it took for him to break, to give in to his desire to claim full possession of her mouth.

Then her hands were in his hair, her own answering passion sweeping away what reason remained. He knew it was a mistake to kiss her, and she had to know it, too, and yet the fact that she couldn't stop any more than he could only fired him with that much more undeniable need.

He savored the feel of her arms around him, the slide of her hands down his back and sides as if feeling every muscle and sinew. He felt his hard arousal, and knew her responding tremble.

Her slender curves felt so right in his arms. His senses reeled and memories rushed him along with a confusion of things that could and couldn't be. All he wanted was to submerge himself inside her and forget the past, the present, and most of all the future. Her soft breasts crushed against his chest and he longed to touch them, put his mouth on them.

For two years, he'd ached and imagined and dreamed of this one sweet woman. Oh, how he'd dreamed of her, with agonizing clarity, and woken to the dread of what his real life had become.

But no dream had been as incredible as this reality. He'd known hunger from the moment he'd spied her in the jungle of Callula Island. It was crazy and dangerous, and he'd been tortured by her very nearness, longing from the first instant to hold her this way.

Now it wasn't a dream; she was real, in his arms, still tormenting him with every whimper, every sigh, every answering arch of her body against his very full need. She was everything he remembered and so much more.

With what lucidity he could find, he tore apart from her. For another beat they stood there, heartbeat to heartbeat.

She stared up at him, looking shaken and lost. Trembling, as he was.

Blood thrummed inside his head. Soul-deep need crushed him with the desire to take her again, to take more than kisses. To take her as a husband took a wife. Divorce papers and the hell of his life be damned. But the painful shimmer in her ravaged gaze struck him, ripped into his heart.

Emotion stabbed him to the marrow, and he had to look away for a moment, break the power of the connection that shouldn't still exist after two years of separation. He *couldn't* allow it to remain.

He shut his eyes for that awful beat, fighting the power of her hold on his heart and mind, even his soul. His head pounded and his body felt as if it were on fire.

When he was certain he had control of himself, he opened his eyes to find her still staring at him, quiet and yet so strong even as she stood before him shaking. He had to protect her, from him most of all, and he was doing a damn bad job of it so far.

"Don't stop," she whispered brokenly.

"If I don't, you know what will happen," he said, stripping his voice of any feeling, pretending he didn't want what she would have given him. Pretending not to care that after the way he'd hurt her, she still would have opened her arms, her body, to him, a monster. In pity.

"And why would that be so terrible? We're still married."

Her voice was so small, and he wanted to take her back into his arms and tell her it would be wonderful, fantastic, and more painful than anything he could imagine.

"It would be wrong, not terrible," he managed with a grim finality. Wrong for her, and wrong for him, too, because he would only want her that much more. Taking Paige once wouldn't be enough. He had to let her go, and he had to let her go without making things any worse than they already were.

The gauze he'd taped to cover the flesh wound on her head was bleeding through the bandage, and guilt squeezed his chest. He scooped her into his arms, giving her no time to resist or even think. There was a certain hell in holding her, and he punished himself with the need it caused.

He deposited her on the pallet in the alcove and turned away.

"Wait." She sat forward, took hold of his hand, pulling him back before he could leave her. "I don't—" She stumbled on her words, her voice vulnerable even as her eyes burned bright and fierce. She touched her mouth briefly, and her fingers trembled even as he saw her will surge in her gaze. "You say you want a divorce. You act as if you can't wait to get rid of me. And then you kiss me like that. Like—"

She broke off, and he was glad. He'd kissed her like a man possessed, a man who needed her and wanted her like he needed and wanted his next breath. It was all true, and it was all equally impossible.

"Forget that ever happened," he said flatly. "It was a mistake. I've been alone for two years. And maybe you're right, maybe I'm just enough of a man still to feel a man's desire. Don't confuse it with anything more." He was speaking to himself as well as her.

He saw the pain, raw in her eyes. But better for her to know pain now than the agony she'd know later if she were to open her heart to him again. He had no future to promise Paige. She let go of his hand.

"Maybe *you're* the one who's right," she said, the pain blazing into fury at his cold words, just as he'd intended. "Maybe you *have* become a monster, after all."

And even though he'd wanted to make her angry, wanted to forge this ice-cold distance between them, her stormy response tore at the heart that was, dammit, all too human still.

He wanted to touch her again so badly, he felt his hands shaking with the unbearable longing to mold his body to hers, to hear those sexy sighs against his lips again, to taste her hope as if he could drink it in and make it his own.

"You're bleeding through the bandage," he said flatly. "Your wound needs tending then you need to rest."

He would get more gauze, clean her wound, tend her, and then he would stay as far away from her as possible. She'd made him feel, for one shocking, shining moment, that he really was a man again, whole and free. She'd made him feel more alive than he'd felt since his life had exploded along with his lab. She'd touched him as if he weren't a monster. But it had been nothing more than an illusion that would shatter all too easily.

He was more monster than man.

And if he'd made her understand that now, then he'd done one thing right today. She thought all he had to fear were terrorists. He only wished that were true.

Paige didn't know there was a traitor in PAX. She thought *he* was the one she couldn't quite trust. If all of this was true… She'd trusted him too easily once. And she was a hell of a lot safer not completely trusting him now. She'd go on with her new life outside PAX.

And he'd do what he had to do even if it cost him his life. But he'd be damned if it would cost Paige's, too.

She watched him walk away. The sound of her treacherous heart beat loud in her ears, more thunderous than the wind outside the cave. She'd known from the instant she'd laid eyes on Kieran that he had changed, but the haunting emptiness and deadly energy of him now stunned her. The darkness inside him was taking over the tender man he'd been.

But was that darkness the wolf side growing stronger, or something in many ways worse? What if everything he was telling her was a lie? Something deep inside her twisted and she didn't want to even consider it.

What if he was working with the terrorists and he had made up this story of his betrayal to stop her from turning him in? The possibilities tangled in her mind along with the terrible wonder of his kiss.

His words afterward had been deliberately calculated to cause her pain, and so had her own. Was this all that was left of the love they'd once shared? Was he truly this shell of a man he wanted her to see? Or were there more truths he was hiding from her?

I did everything in my power to protect you, Paige.

His words just before he'd told her about the contamination with the activation serum rolled back into her mind. She felt confused and sick and afraid to even think they meant anything that mattered to her heart.

Always, Kieran had sought to protect her. It had often frustrated her to the point of argument, and some of the most bitter battles of their marriage had been waged over risks she'd taken in the League's covert organization in testing underwater communication technologies. And yet even when they'd argued over her work, she'd known it was fear and love that drove him. He'd never recovered from the day he'd watched his sister Annelie slip from his hands, swept away into that raging river. He'd rarely spoken of the tragedy, but she knew he blamed himself.

Now he was protecting Paige, again, and she was as frustrated as she'd ever been. Even when she knew how implacable he could be, she couldn't give up without a fight. No wonder how cold he was to her now, she had known a different Kieran. And that Kieran still lived. She saw him deep behind those haunted eyes. She saw him in the wolves painted wild and free on these cave walls.

Then he was back. The cave's alcove shrank by the mere fact of his return. She wanted to tell him she'd tend her own wound, but fatigue drenched her. She felt emotionally drained as much as anything else. Seeing Kieran again… She hadn't been ready for it. And she had to pull herself together. Someone had sent that pilot today. They could send someone else tomorrow. Whatever the truth was behind Kieran's life on this island, she had to be prepared for anything, but the last thing she knew how to prepare herself for was Kieran's touch.

His hands were as efficient as they were startlingly gentle. He sat beside her to remove the blood-damp gauze bandage on her temple. He'd brought a bowl with some water and a cloth, and lightly he smoothed it over her skin, cleaning the wound. When he was finished, he taped fresh gauze over the injury. Harsh lines carved his face with his own fatigue. There was a look about him that made her think he was in some kind of pain, not emotional but physical. She wondered again how he had survived so long without the containment serum…

And how much longer he could survive without it.

She tried to not look at him as he worked. The wolves painted on the rock above her drew her eyes again. Kieran's spirit seemed to flow out of them onto the rough surface. Then she realized looking at Kieran's art was almost as painful as looking into his eyes.

He finished tending her wound, and she felt bereft as he removed his touch. His fingers were warm, calloused, and somehow reassuring.

"Lay down. Go to sleep, Paige."

"What about you?" she asked, realizing only then that she was in what must be his bed, the place he'd slept for two long years while she had lain in her lonely bed without him.

"I'm better off awake." And in that instant, she saw the vulnerability inside him spring to the surface in spite of his hard shield. All this time, he'd been alone on this island. And if what he'd told her about his contamination was true… He could die. She couldn't be angry, not after that thought.

"Why?" she asked. "What happens if you sleep?"

A long beat slid in the taut gloam. "I dream."

She swallowed thickly. "You're not alone tonight. If you dream, I'll be there."

He made a bitter sound. "Don't start thinking you can save me, Paige. Don't imagine that I'm anything but what I am. I hurt you—badly." His already severe features tightened further. "I wish it could have been different, but it's not and it won't be."

Her heart clenched. "That's what you keep saying," she said carefully, watching his face, wishing for some sign of what thoughts he secreted in his mind. "Is it me you're trying to convince, or you?" The words hung there in the thick shadows. She thought of the photograph he'd kept in that book all this time.

A shadow passed over his dark eyes, so quickly she wondered if she'd truly seen it at all. The shield slid back into place.

"I've had two years to accept who I am," he said. "You're the one who's having trouble dealing with the truth."

"I know that our marriage is over," she said, and she could hear the strain in her own voice, fought the emotion that swelled in her throat. "But I don't want anger to be all that's left between us. Not after everything we've been through together."

She'd spent two years trying to excise him from her heart. Amputating a limb would have been easier.

She went on in a voice that she steadied by sheer grit. "If you think I could ever trust my heart to you again, you're more wrong than you know." And if she was lying to herself along with him, that was just fine. She was better off in her fantasy world where she couldn't fall for Kieran again. "I'm starting over now. I want a different life. Dinner on time in a suburban tract home, soccer games with the kids. A minivan." It was beyond the reach of her imagination to see Kieran in such an ordinary world. "But that doesn't mean we have to be enemies now. It doesn't mean you have to be alone."

He didn't say anything about the normal life she'd just described. She wondered if he believed her. Sometimes she wondered if she believed herself.

"I'm used to being alone," was all he said.

"So am I," she said, and damn him, her voice cracked just a little. "I've been alone for two years, too." She'd been in the hell he'd left her in. She drew in a choked breath.

His voice burned low in the night. "I'm sorry for that, Paige. More than you know."

Her heart thumped hard in her chest. Somehow his sympathy was worse than his coldness. The truth was she didn't know what she wanted from him. And the scary thing was that she wanted anything at all from a man she couldn't trust.

His dark eyes held hers for a long second then he

moved to tug the rumpled blanket from the foot of the pallet where she'd left it earlier. He tucked it around her and she leaned back. It was awkward and sweet and painful all at once. Jagged emotions tore inside her. She'd made a mistake to let him kiss her, a mistake to offer more. She'd revealed herself, opened herself too much to man who wouldn't open himself to her at all.

She closed her eyes only because she couldn't bear to see him watching her with those enigmatic, haunted depths. It was little use. She felt his heat, smelled his masculine scent, heard his almost imperceptible breaths...the same way she had felt his presence every night for two years no matter how far away he'd been then.

He didn't leave her alone. And she promised herself she wouldn't wonder why as the sound of howling wind penetrated the cave walls.

Paige actually slept. She was surprised when she woke. Her mouth felt dry, her body ached, but when she stretched, she felt the renewed strength in her limbs. She looked at her watch and saw it was early. Outside the cave, she heard nothing but thick stillness. The eye of the storm. However, they would still have to wait for the second wave of Hurricane Bernadette to pass before it would be safe to fly out.

Across the cave, she saw Kieran. He sat in a chair

at the work table, his back to her. She sat up, relieved to find the lightheaded feeling from the night before was gone. All she felt now was hungry. Some food and she would be fine.

Or as fine as she could be when she was trapped on a stormy island wondering who would come gunning for them next, with a man who pulled her and pushed her away all at once.

For long moments she lay there taking in everything that had happened. She still had so many questions. And she might only have a few hours left to get any of the answers.

She got up and padded softly across the cave. Her shoes were placed neatly by her rain slicker against the cave wall. Kieran had apparently removed them when he'd first carried her into the cave after she'd been shot. The rock floor of the cave felt cold on her bare skin despite the warmth generated by the heater. As she reached Kieran, he let out a low curse.

Blood sprang out on his jaw and she realized he had cut himself shaving. She tensed for an instant. He was cleaning up his unkempt appearance. He was planning to do something with the information she'd brought, and whatever it was, he didn't want to tell her.

He'd made it clear he wouldn't go to PAX for help, and she didn't understand why. It made her furious and scared for him at the same time. He needed the serum. Was he going to break in to get it? It was wrong and dangerous, and she wanted to take him by those broad shoulders and shake him for his stupidity.

"Here," she said and she reached for a towel on the table to stanch the flow of blood from the tiny cut. He was using a knife to shave, and a pair of scissors lay nearby. She could see he'd already cut the beard close before he'd begun to shave. "Let me help," she said. "I'm surprised you haven't bled to death already." And in fact she could see he had cut himself more than once with his far too simple shaving tools.

There was only one chair in the cave, so she quickly pulled over a crate, sat and leaned toward him, close. The fresh soapy male scent of him teased her senses, and the drawn, sleepless lines of his mysterious eyes touched her heart. She knew the intense desire to kiss him like she had last night.

God, he had felt so good to her, so familiar and gloriously right no matter how wrong her head knew him to be. He made her lose her wild fear, lose her sanity, lose everything, just by putting his hard mouth on hers. How could a man who thought himself a monster feel down deep to her so extraordinarily, sensually, safe? Just thinking about that kiss strung her nerves so taut, she could barely think.

She forced herself to focus on the simple task of placing her hand over his to take the knife. His gaze shot to her.

"I'm doing fine on my own," he said with those

hot, heavy eyes of his that made her stomach drop. Damn him for having that power over her no matter how she tried to steel her will against him.

"If you're going back to civilization," she probed, "I'm guessing you don't want to attract attention by looking like a mountain man. But you don't want to look like something straight from a horror movie, either, which you will if you keep at it. I can do a better job."

He looked annoyed, which he usually did when she was making sense on a topic about which he wanted to argue. It was, in fact, the same expression he'd had on his face when she'd proposed marriage to him. He'd been the slow and thoughtful one while she'd been impatient. He'd always held a part of himself back from her, that part of him that was so damaged by his past. And he'd held it back even after they'd wed. In truth, she'd always known that with his background, he had never quite believed he could have a normal life while she'd been overeager to claim one.

But the life they'd built together had been anything but ordinary. She'd come to Callula Island hoping it would be the beginning of a *real* normal life. Without Kieran. Without PAX. She couldn't count how many new starts she'd made in her life. Not one of them had worked out yet.

She'd been ten when her parents had died. Cute

babies got adopted, not confused, gangly pre-pubescents. Foster home after foster home had been one new start after another, never ending quite how she hoped.

Her marriage hadn't, either.

Always, she'd put her whole heart and soul into every new relationship. Always, she'd given away her trust. Always, it had been trampled in return.

And if she repeated those mistakes again, she would get what she deserved. So why was it so hard for her to walk away from Kieran now?

"Still the same Paige," Kieran said and something quirked at the corner of his mouth as she took the knife. "Pushy." He steadied his dark expression as if it was almost too painful to smile, and she slid the blade over his skin.

"I'm not pushy," she said seriously. "I'm right and you still don't like to admit it."

And she was right about going to PAX for help, but she had no idea how to convince him. If he was planning to break in to steal the serum, it would only make everything worse if they caught him. And they'd probably catch him. Especially if he tried to do it alone.

What if she helped him? The idea stung her mind. It went against every principle, every belief, by which she lived her life. And she would be ruined as well as he if they were caught. She didn't even know if he was telling her the truth. She still felt as if he was hiding something from her.

He watched her, and this close, she could feel his eyes even though she kept her own attention directed at the clean swipe of the blade as she drew it over his jaw with care, wiping the cut stubble between scrapes against the towel.

The motion of her fingers on the cold metal sliding against his warm skin was almost erotic. He had a lean, interesting face, handsome in a classic way that had always brought attention, and yet at the same time, it was imperfect. He'd told her once that he'd broken his nose in a fight when he was nine years old, and it had a slight bump that made it not quite straight. He had a scar from a car accident over one brow. The accident in which his sister Annelie had drowned.

And always, his eyes had been dangerous, serious, intense. His deep umber-brown gaze had never been a comfortable one, and with the hollow fire that burned around the edges now, it was that much more intimidating.

As she worked, she revealed the old Kieran—clean-shaven, younger than the bearded wild man had seemed to be, and somehow vulnerable despite the unyielding lines of his features. She used the cloth to clear off the remains of the lather, and sat back.

Her heart squeezed at the painful familiarity of

him now. *This* was the Kieran she knew, the Kieran she had loved and trusted with her whole heart.

And that Kieran was no monster.

"You're not going to get far with that helicopter, you know," she said quietly. "You'll need a car, gas, food... And to break into PAX, you'll need me."

He caught her gaze on that last word. She held his look steady for a long beat then turned to pick up the scissors.

"You need a haircut, too," she added.

"No," he clipped out.

She ignored him, pretended to examine his hair. "Don't worry. One of my foster moms had one of those long-haired guinea pigs. She let me cut its hair once. I'm experienced."

Kieran didn't crack a smile, not even a tip of his hard lips this time.

"This isn't funny, Paige. And I'm not talking about you cutting my hair."

"I know."

He reached up and grasped the fist in which she held the scissors. "You're pushing, Paige. And it isn't going to work." His resolute gaze pinned her as much as his grip. "You're leaving PAX. Our marriage is over. This is none of your affair now."

She watched his eyes and even in their hard fire, she saw how he shuttered them against her. "What are you hiding from me?" Her mind clicked on links, trying to make a connection. "How did you know that PAX thought you'd been in on the plot with Phil?"

The story hadn't been in the media. The PAX League didn't release stories to the press, not about their most secret work. And she knew he'd never contacted anyone in PAX.

He'd simply disappeared.

"Don't ask questions, Paige. You don't want the answers." His grip on her hand tightened as if he were willing her to stop, but he was incredibly wrong, she did want answers.

"Where did you get the cash that's in that chest?" Her thoughts stumbled, hit pay dirt. "You wouldn't have taken it from Dub. You probably gave Dub money, not the other way around." They'd always kept emergency cash in that lockbox in the apartment, where the serum had been found. "You came back and took that money from the lockbox that night—or that morning, before I woke up."

He'd been in the apartment, while she'd been asleep. He hadn't said goodbye. The pain was a heavy ache inside her that she couldn't let herself dwell on now. She shoved it aside, focused on her need for answers with her scientist's mind.

"There was no money ever taken from our bank accounts," she continued. "I know that." That morning was an awful nightmare. She'd woken to Vinn's phone call— "You were there when Vinn called."

Something desperate flared in his eyes.

"You're wrong."

He let go of her hand, stood and strode away from her. She was on the right track.

"No, I'm not." Her heart pounded. The scissors clattered on the table as she threw them down and went after him. "And if you were there, if you took cash out of the lockbox, that means the serum wasn't there then. You wouldn't have left the serum behind. You already knew you needed it. But it was there, PAX found it." Her thoughts spun. "It wasn't someone from the terrorist network who set you up." The full ramification shattered into her mind. "It was someone in PAX."

Oh, God, if this was true—

He turned, and the look on his face had her heart pounding all the harder. Pain spilled out in his hard voice.

"You don't know what you've done now, Paige. You don't know how much danger you're in."

"I know how much danger *you're* in!" she cried wildly, still trying to wrap her mind around the mind-blowing implications of the story she'd put together. The puzzle of that awful night had haunted her all this time, and it was even worse than she'd imagined. At the same time, she knew an awesome relief.

If this was true… It explained so much. Kieran had been set up and now she knew how.

It settled over her in a strange calm. “We’re both in danger,” she said. “And we’re in this together.”

Chapter 5

No, no, and no. They weren't in this together. But Kieran knew that determined light in Paige's eyes. She thought she could help him. And the thought of her even trying brought on dread, swift and immediate.

"I don't want your help, Paige," he said firmly. "You're going to disappear somewhere safe until this is over."

"No." The refusal burst from her. "We have to go back to PAX. We have to tell them the truth."

"No one is going to believe my story, Paige." His bitter words rang true whether she liked them or not.

He needed her to see that. "They wouldn't have believed me two years ago, and they're even less likely to believe me today. I ran, remember?"

"But you have to have the serum, and you have to tell them about the traitor. There's no choice now. We have to go back!"

"*I* have to go back, Paige. Not you. End of discussion." He stalked past her to his work table. He had to prepare to leave, and he knew the cave would be found and searched. They knew about Callula Island now. He had to destroy everything that might lead the traitor to the serum's secrets.

And then he would destroy the traitor. And Paige— Paige would be somewhere safe, where she could have that normal life she craved, go to soccer practices in that minivan.

Outside, the wind picked up as he began pouring out beakers and vials. Across the cave, he could hear Paige pace toward him, feel the restless anger emanating from her as she neared. Sharply honed survival instincts warned him not to turn.

"Do you think I can just go somewhere and hide when you're in trouble?" she cried.

He refused to turn, refused to meet her impatient demand. Refused to be pulled in by her sweet, insistent hope.

The last thing he wanted was for Paige to be in on this horror with him. He had spent two years learning how to think like a man with no future, an animal. This was not the time to stop.

And yet he couldn't stop thinking like a man. A man who wanted Paige safe.

He'd lost everything that had once chipped away at the walls he'd kept around his heart for so long. At PAX, he'd gained a sort of family like he'd never known. He'd had a father in PAX chief Vinn Regan whom he could respect, a team of agents who were always on his side. He'd had the beginnings of real hope then. Hell, he'd even married Paige. He'd thought he'd cheated destiny. For one brief shining moment he'd found his little version of Camelot with Paige and PAX.

But destiny had caught up to him. His agency family had let him down. And all he'd been able to do for Paige was disappear before he robbed her of the future she could still have without him. The future she'd always been crazy enough to believe in so much more than him.

He wanted her to have that future. He didn't want her to die.

"Don't you dare shut me out." She grabbed his arm in her strong hold and pulled him to face her. "Don't you dare expect me to walk away."

He winced at the betrayal and confusion in her eyes. It hurt, just as he'd known it would.

"It's not me they tried to kill yesterday, Paige," he

said roughly, worry for her banding his chest. "It was you." He'd spent the entire, sleepless night thinking about it. "They don't want *me* dead. They came here to *capture* me, not kill me." He waited a beat, watched his words sink in, prayed she'd accept them. "You were right about that, they haven't forgotten about me—they want the secrets of the serums. That pilot shot you, Paige. I don't think it was a mistake.

"They tracked you to me," he went on. "You were expendable after that." God, she was expendable *now.* There was no reason for them to let her live, and plenty of reasons for them to want her dead. "Whoever was in on this plot with Phil wanted to sell the research. Why should that have changed? They still want to sell the research. They have a buyer, but the research is gone. The project was closed. The activation serum was burned up in the lab. The containment serum has no value without the activation serum. They need me alive."

His words hung heavy in the cave. Outside, there was a rush of wind. The eye of the storm had passed. They had a few more hours to wait then it would be safe to escape the island.

"You can't get into PAX without me," she persisted. "You can't get past the security. I'm still in the system. My resignation isn't final yet."

PAX security was set up on advanced biometric face, finger, and iris scans to authenticate individuals passing from the main, public areas of the PAX League building into the secret headquarters that contained the laboratories and offices of PAX's covert operations.

"I'm betting I can," he said. "They would have left my code intact, on a trigger, in case I ever came back."

"Then they'll catch you!" Her voice was sharp and frightened, her face drained of all color.

"I'll be ready for them," he said grimly. "There's got to be a trail. They can't have been depending on me all this time. Someone's already working on the serum." He'd spent the long night thinking about that, too. Someone who already had a deal with a foreign agency would be working on the serum on their own. Working in the dark, and probably desperate by now. "But they've failed—if they hadn't, they wouldn't still want me. Files, chemicals, all would have had to be checked out. And who would have noticed? No one knows there's a traitor inside PAX. No one expects anyone to be working on the serum." But he did. And he'd find the damning evidence. There had to be cash involved, too. A lot of cash. And he had an idea how to work on that angle, too.

Paige grabbed hold of his arm, wouldn't let him push her away. "Use *my* bio-read to get in."

"That's tailgating, Paige. They'd know you helped me."

"I don't care."

Hurricane-force winds outside the cave filled the pin-drop silence inside. Kieran wheeled away, but not before Paige saw the torment in his expression.

She took a ragged breath and went after him.

"I'll claim you forced me to use my bio-read to get into headquarters," she went on heatedly. "No one would believe that I would help you willingly. Not after what you did to me."

That hurt. She saw the flinch in those shuttered eyes. And she wished she hadn't had to say it, but she knew it was true. Everyone at PAX knew just how much she wanted to move on with her life. She'd done a damn fine job of convincing even her closest friends that she was through with Kieran. But how could she really be through when she still cared this much?

"And that's why I won't let you help me, Paige. Not after what I did to you."

Her own words hurt her just as much when they were returned to her. He was cutting her out, just like that. Again, dammit. "You won't make it," she whispered, her voice raw.

"I got out of PAX before. I can get out again. Whatever happens, I'm not going to be locked up."

Something in his face scared her then and she began to shake. Something so detached and dead. His plan was too dangerous, and she had a feeling he'd do anything before he let himself be locked up. Even die. She reached up, briefly touched his clean-shaven face, the skin surprisingly soft in spite of his features' harsh carve. He was all darkly tanned flesh and solid muscle, but under it all lay a heart she didn't want to stop beating. A heart that was more tender than he would let her see now.

"I know you think you have no future, but I don't buy it," she cried desperately. "The Kieran I knew wasn't a quitter."

His long look was dark, and she knew what he was thinking. He was not the Kieran she'd known. And yet… She couldn't forget the man he'd once been. She couldn't forget that he'd once meant everything to her and that he'd made her believe she meant everything to him.

How foolish she'd been to think she could.

"I'm not quitting, Paige. I'm doing the right thing. And I have to do it on my own."

He sounded stubbornly noble, relentlessly protective. He had always had a sense of honor that had made what they said he'd done too hard to believe. It had been one of the things she'd loved about him, but now she only hated him for it.

She hated his remoteness, too, and that feeling wasn't new. She'd accused him once of having no feelings, though she'd known it wasn't true. He had feelings. But they were so rarely shared that after three years of marriage, she'd only begun to understand him.

And any hope of that changing now was more lost than ever. Kieran had erected an emotional force field around himself in the two years he'd spent on Callula Island. He'd never been an easy man to know, and he would be an impossible one now.

There would be no do-overs when it came to their relationship. But she didn't want him to give up. She wanted him to make it out of this thing alive, and she wanted him to want it, too.

"Don't do this," she pleaded. "You don't have to be a hero."

Seconds dragged into minutes. She could feel the heat of his body washing hers, the animal-like hum of his energy. She wanted to take comfort in his readiness, but it was his readiness that filled her with fear.

She could see, for just a second, the emotion in his eyes he quickly shuttered. And she knew with a sick dread in the pit of her stomach that it didn't matter what she said. He'd made up his mind. He was convinced that he had to take down the traitor alone. Horror shuddered through her.

"There's only one thing you can do to help me," he said grimly. "I need to know the names of every agent who was in our apartment the day after the explosion. And then you're going to disappear."

Julius Kelley. David Rodale. Brigitte Perry. Kent Oberman. Shay Masterson. This was the team of

PAX agents Vinn Regan had led into their downtown apartment building the morning after the explosion. And they knew too damn little about most of them.

"Talia was there, too," Paige added. "She wasn't on-site in any official capacity, of course." Shadows flitted about the hollows of her face as she spoke of that terrible day.

Talia Regan, the PAX chief's daughter as well as a fellow agent, would have been there for Paige, to lend her support. Kieran worked to keep his mind on track, not veer into the emotional abyss of imagining how difficult that day had been for Paige. He focused on analyzing the players in this deadly game as he paced the confines of the cave. Paige had cut his hair—and with his shoulder-length mane gone and his newly shaven face, he felt lighter and unfamiliar to himself. He wasn't a stranger to Paige, though.

After he'd been shaved, she'd looked at him in that way he remembered all too sharply. As if he were an attractive man, a man who made her blood pound for all the right reasons instead of all the wrong ones he knew he inspired now.

And for that tenuous beat, he'd wished more than anything that he could turn back the clock to that day before he'd gone to work, before the explosion. He'd made love to Paige with all the tender urgency he'd always known when they'd been intimate. He remembered how she'd climaxed with her eyes wide open, so giving and sweet. They'd had breakfast on the balcony of their sixth floor river-view apartment—then she'd stripped bare, pulled him onto the low cushioned chaise where they were hidden by the tightly built railing, and made him late for work.

In the grim shelter of his primitive cave on this morning two years later, he'd whipped up a breakfast that he'd silently handed Paige while he'd fought to laser out any remnant of memory from that last meal they'd shared on the balcony where they'd made love.

But he knew better than to let himself be drawn back into that world that no longer existed for him. He'd pushed back his plate, having forced himself to eat past the choked, intolerable emotion in his throat, and begun to pace as they went down the list of agents who'd entered their apartment that fateful morning.

He and Paige had met Talia in their early days at PAX. Like most PAX agents, they had been first hired in to the agency's outer layer of global good works. The agency sought the finest graduates to carry out international case studies and fact-finding assignments to areas of armed conflict, engineering and technical support for post-conflict rebuilding, medical and charitable missions to underdeveloped countries, and environmental and scientific research into climate destabilization and biological diversity around the world.

The research that went on within the League's secret headquarters prepared agents to fight PAX's deeper battle—global terror. After signing on with PAX, agent candidates underwent the psychological and physical observations and testing required before individuals were selected into the secret core of the League. Further and more rigorous analysis targeted agents for paranormal activation.

Paige had joined a team pushing the boundaries of human existence underwater. Talia worked on a radioactivity immunity project. And Kieran became part of the wolf/human ectoplasmic research. Recruited in close succession, they'd become fast friends.

"We've known Talia for years—" Paige started. The edge of her voice bordered on desperation.

"We knew Phil for years, too," Kieran broke in. Sometimes he still couldn't wrap his mind around the idea that his partner had intended to sell out their research, and he'd spent long months afterward trying to convince himself it couldn't be true. The hell of it was, he didn't know. Now he had to wonder if Phil had been set up, too. All he knew was that if Phil *had* done it, he hadn't done it alone.

"She's my best friend."

"We can't look at this emotionally, Paige," Kieran

reminded her, hating that it was necessary. "Everyone's a suspect. Including Talia."

He could see the bitter denial in her eyes, but she held back from saying anything more. Paige hadn't had the time he'd had to detach from their fellow agents. Nothing about this situation would be easy for her. She wanted to see the best in everyone.

She sat there for a long moment, then spoke again. "Shay, David and Kent did the initial search. Brigitte arrived late— I'm not sure if it was before or after the serum was discovered. Julius was in charge of the team."

He knew the PAX agents would have fanned out in the apartment, worked with precise and efficient speed. The internal task force was comprised of skilled forensic and investigative specialists, most of which operated in isolation from the other agents to better enable them to probe with objective clarity.

"They must have grilled you about me," he said.

She nodded. "But there wasn't anything I could tell them. There was nothing leading up to the explosion to make me think you were planning anything like that."

"Do they know that you didn't believe the frame?"

"I told them I couldn't believe you'd been involved in the plot with Phil. But the evidence—"

It had been damning, more damning than he'd even known at the time.

"At first I was adamant about your innocence," she said. "But later…" Her voice trailed off and he could see her gathering strength before she continued. "Later it was just too painful. When you never came back or even tried to get in touch with me— I got angry. And they knew that, too. And I stopped trying to convince anyone that you were innocent. They knew I was through with our marriage, that I wanted a divorce."

Her eyes shadowed and she glanced away for a taut moment. "I had to move on with my life. I decided to leave PAX, then Talia—"

"What about Talia?"

Her gaze lifted. "She thought I should confront you. She thought I couldn't move on without facing you."

"She urged you to find me."

"She knew how difficult it was for me after you left. Vinn and Talia both have treated me like family, taken me under their wing, made sure I wasn't alone for holidays, or alone for anything."

The PAX chief had been like family to Kieran, too. The only real father figure he'd ever known. The chief's acceptance of his guilt tore at Kieran's soul every day.

This was the chief who'd hired in a young college graduate who'd pulled himself up by his bootstraps from a past that included a criminal record. Vinn had believed in him, though. Till the lab and his life had exploded. Then Vinn had stopped believing.

Paige would have been a whole lot better off if she'd been back at PAX believing he was a traitor, too. Now she was in danger because of him. As brilliant as her mind was, as practical as she could be in her work, she was a dreamer at heart, always hoping for the best.

It was important now that he be very careful to not give her any reason to think she could hold out any hope for him. She would only end up hurt that way.

He recognized frustration burning in her eyes even now as they went down the list of task force members. She thought he was shutting her out.

She didn't understand how treacherously close he was to doing the complete opposite. He had to force himself to detach every time he looked at her. Leaving Paige two years ago had been the most painful decision of his life.

Now he had to do it all over again, as soon as he could get her some place safe.

"I got to know Brigitte last year," Paige told him. "She left full-time work with PAX not too long after the investigation. She was on a case where a child was orphaned and she just fell in love with the little girl. She became her foster mother, and I think she's adopted the girl now. They still call her in occasionally for consulting, but that's it. She came to me one day and wanted to know what it had been like to be in foster care. I don't really know anything about

Kent Oberman," she added, thinking down the list. "But he's been on the task force for years and has a fine reputation."

"Julius Kelley was in our training group," Kieran said. Kelley had seemed like a solid agent, disciplined and decent. But who knew? One of these fine, decent, disciplined agents was working with a foreign terrorist network. "What do you know about Shay Masterson?"

"I've gotten to know him better than the others." Paige combed tense fingers through her hair, pushing back the wispy tendrils that covered the wound on her temple. "He would come around pretty often, ask if I'd remembered anything else or had heard from you. He was incredibly persistent." She looked away for a minute.

Kieran sat down on the crate. He'd given her the one chair while he'd prepared their simple breakfast. "Persistent how?"

Paige turned her gaze back to him. "He seemed to think I knew where you were. He called, came by, sometimes daily at first, then at least once a week later on."

Something akin to jealousy spiraled through Kieran's chest. Masterson's persistence seemed over the top, just as his own reaction of possessiveness was. He could easily see Masterson, or any other living, breathing man, going after Paige, and he had no right now to object, even if he didn't like it. He filed away the possibility that Masterson could have had a much darker motivation for continuing to visit Paige and prepared to move on.

"David Rodale is dead," Paige said then.

Kieran did a double take. "What happened to him?"

"His family was killed in an awful traffic accident. I don't remember all the details. He was a mess. I saw him at the office a few weeks later. He tried to come back to work, but he was devastated. They put him on leave, and—"

"What?"

"He shot himself. They found him in his home. It had been a few days and... It was just horrible."

Kieran's gut twisted. He'd barely met Rodale, but he remembered seeing him at one of the League's charitable events once with his family. A pretty wife with two pretty little girls. Now they were all dead.

The traitor in PAX was still alive. But he couldn't stop wondering if David Rodale's family tragedy was somehow connected.

He didn't want what had happened to David Rodale's family to happen to Paige. His heart twisted.

"You think that wasn't an accident now, don't you?" she whispered thinly. "You think David Rodale might have been involved. Maybe he was going to talk. Maybe they killed his family as a warning."

He was silent for a moment then he looked up at

her again. "Maybe if I hadn't run away two years ago, they'd still be alive."

Paige gasped. "No. You had no idea. You aren't responsible for their deaths."

But somewhere deep inside, he felt responsible. Paige was right when she said he'd done the wrong thing two years ago. He'd give his life now to fix it if he had to.

They had their list. One of these people had planted the evidence to frame Kieran and now wanted the formula for the activation serum. Either that person—or Kieran—could be about to die for it.

And the sooner he could narrow down this list, the better.

Outside the cave, the wind had softened its rage. The worst of the storm had passed, and it could be too late if they waited for perfect conditions. They'd been talking for hours, and now the time for talk was done.

"It's time to go now," he said, and she nodded and stood.

Never had she looked more hauntingly fragile to him, despite the steely strength he knew formed her spine. Her life lay in his hands. There was a very real danger approaching the island.

He could feel the danger, sense it, in the humming pressure building in his blood. The pressure to shift built inside him, and resisting that pressure was nearly impossible and always painful. It was harder now than it had been in the beginning, and combined with the increasing bouts of pain he experienced at other times, he had almost forgotten what it was like to feel normal.

The containment serum would give him the immutable control he so lacked now—it would take away the pain and ensure that he could always come back from the change. He had to pray that he could physically and mentally withstand the urge to shift once they left the cave. He had to—for Paige.

She couldn't fly that chopper out of here alone.

Chapter 6

They got their things together quickly. Kieran took little. Two years on Callula Island and he prepared to walk out of the cave that had been his home with nothing more than the cash, his logbook, the laptop, the gun, and the clothes on his back. He left the supplies, equipment, and chemicals behind after pouring the mixtures out from the beakers. The terrorist network could determine nothing from what remained, not without his data.

He shrugged into a windbreaker and looked back just before leaving the cave. But he wasn't looking at the place he'd spent two long, lonesome years. He was looking at her, something fierce in his expression.

There was no knowing what they'd encounter on the beach. Her pulsebeat kicked up a notch at the prospect of what could be waiting for them.

"Ready?" he asked with quiet intensity.

No, she wasn't ready. She stood there, a wave of panic washing over her. She didn't panic often. She was a trained, steady professional.

But even as she tried to put on a front that this was business, it wasn't. It was all too personal. Kieran could die. So could she.

"I'm ready as I'll ever be," she answered, and damn it, moisture pricked her eyes. She averted her gaze, blinked swiftly and gathered her strength.

Then Kieran's finger touched her chin, and she met his deep, unwavering gaze again. Her heart pounded so hard and fast, she knew he must be able to hear it over the wind still whistling outside the cave. Heat flooded her cold skin and every pulse point throbbed. He'd told her to forget that kiss had ever happened, but she knew then that he hadn't forgotten it.

His eyes flared and with no word, he pulled her to him and swallowed the soft gasp she made against his mouth. Her breasts pressed against him as he nudged her body closer, and the tender fire of his physical need for her annihilated every thought of fear. The kiss took her sweetly, hotly, fully.

He rocked against her, tangling his hands hungrily in her hair, and all the anguish in her bones seemed to melt away beneath his passionate claim. He tasted like lost dreams and some potent drug, and she had the feeling twenty gunmen could be waiting outside and it wouldn't matter as long as he was kissing her. She never wanted him to stop. He plundered and ravished, needy, and she was just as needy in return.

Then he dragged his lips away from hers. Her hand had settled instinctively on his chest and she could feel that dangerous heart he didn't want her to think he had anymore, thundering as much as her own. Dark, aroused eyes locked with hers and she could see the struggle in those impermeable depths.

"Paige—"

And still he stood there, just looking at her. Maybe he was as confused by the energy still thrumming between them as she was.

She wished he would kiss her, touch her, again. She wished she could stop wishing.

And she knew she couldn't blame him for her useless need for him. He hadn't promised her anything. In fact, he'd done the complete opposite.

He went on carefully. "I just wanted you to know, before we leave here—"

What? What did he want her to know?

His gaze cloaked, turned unreadable now. He was

a genius at reclaiming control. Her heart hammered with the painful reminder that she couldn't do the same.

"—that I want you to be happy. I want you to be okay. I hurt you, and I want you to let that go and move on with your life, your future. I'm sorry about the way things worked out between us."

He wanted her to move on with her life. He wanted her to be *okay.* And she'd wanted all of that, too. Just yesterday. But all she could think now was that he'd just kissed her *goodbye.*

Then he left no more time for her to think, or to respond—even if she could get over the bitter grief in her throat. Backpack slung over his shoulder, he led her out of the cave.

The wind whipped at them as they emerged from the dim confines of the shelter. The aftereffects of the storm were stunning. Trees twisted, ravaged, bent sideways.

Paige hugged her arms around herself, holding the rain parka close, and looked at Kieran. His see-all eyes sharpened as he glanced around for any sign of lurking danger. Despite the fact that the storm had barely passed, they weren't safe on Callula.

They were dealing with desperate people. Desperate people who could already have arrived. Her pulse strummed as he gave her a nod that told her they were okay. For now.

Together, they tore through the woods, heading for

the leeward beach and the helicopter. Paige prayed they'd find it and that it would be in working order. In truth, she had no idea what they would do if it was not.

In the surreal thickness of the storm-ravaged maritime forest jungle, she felt as if they were running through a nightmare. The forest would never end. They would just keep running forever—

Led by Kieran, they took a much more direct route than her original hike into the barrier island the day before. He knew this island like the back of his hand.

As they moved to lower ground, the aftermath of the storm lessened, and she knew hope that the helicopter might have survived in its protected location. Swampy wood gave way to sand, and through the trees, phantasmal clouded light sparkled off the treacherous wind-tossed sea.

The helicopter sat in the shelter of the beach. The high, rocky ground and cliffs of the opposite side of the island had saved it along with the blessed fact that the hurricane had been a relatively weak one. Sheer relief all but had Paige's knees collapsing.

She burst past Kieran, hope coursing hot through her bloodstream.

"The helicopter looks—"

He pulled her back into the shadows of the tangled wood. His jaw was tight and bunched. Breath jammed in her throat.

"What is it?" She hadn't seen anything but the

beautiful, undamaged helicopter. They could fly out of here.

Kieran's eyes had seen more. And then she understood. A cold anxiety washed through her and her pulse skittered dizzily. His powers of eyesight were far stronger than her own, his wolf sense's stronger than any normal human's could ever be.

She turned quickly. A dark form, quickly growing, came toward the beach through those choppy, gun-gray waters. With her own mortal vision, she couldn't see more than that it was a boat. New desperation vaulted through her. They had reached the beach with seconds to spare.

Her heart kicked, hard.

Kieran made a rapid assessment. "They have automatic weapons." His eyes met hers now for one tortured beat, then he ordered, "But we have a head start. Run."

Paige took off across the sand. She could barely feel her legs. All she could think was—breathe, run, breathe, run. The helicopter seemed a million miles away and the boat swerving crazily over the tossing waves felt like it was right on top of her.

She prayed they'd make it.

Bullets pinged the beach. She didn't dare look back for Kieran. Lungs burning, she reached the helicopter, tore open the door and threw herself inside. Mere seconds passed as she waited for Kieran.

He slid into the pilot's seat and rammed a key into the ignition. The question speared crazily into her panicked mind— *Where did he get that?* Then she knew better than to ask.

He'd taken it from the dead pilot. Maybe that was where he'd gotten the gun, too.

"Get down," he ordered over the roar of the chopper engine.

She ducked as bullets ripped into the helicopter. In a searing glimpse back as she dove, she saw armed men hitting the beach, their speedboat lurching in the savage waters of the shore. Paige pushed the hair out of her eyes and looked up at Kieran.

His face pinched as if in some kind of inner agony. She could see a feral glow rimming his dark orbs as he applied the torque required to lift the craft into a steep hover. Airborne, he rolled on the throttle and brought the helicopter forward against the wind.

A shot pierced the cabin window and she let out a startled scream. Unrelenting fire pecked at the underbelly of the craft. Kieran's skin seemed to gain an eerie grayish cast, and she squeezed her eyes shut and prayed, then opened them again as the helicopter shuddered under the rush of acceleration.

Then the thunder of shots hitting home disappeared, and she sat up, twisted back. Callula Island shrank behind them, men dotting the beach like angry ants.

"We made it," she breathed.

Kieran said nothing. She saw the brutalized fatigue of his face. His hand shook on the throttle. Horror streaked back, flashing through the relief.

"What's wrong?" she asked him, fear rising in her throat.

The gray of his skin had turned to something pale and sick. There was sweat on his brow, and at the same time, he was shivering as if he were freezing.

"Are you all right?" she cried, more scared than she'd been when they were still on the beach. He looked as if he was fighting a demon, and she realized with a shock that he was, and it was the demon inside.

The composure she'd been grappling for crumbled.

Taut, helpless beats passed in which he still didn't answer. She had no idea what to do, how to help him. The hell of it was she was sure she couldn't do anything at all. Ocean sped by beneath them, vast and tempestuous.

At last his stark, soulless gaze lifted from the control panel to hers. She barely recognized his pain-racked voice.

"We're losing fuel. They got the tank."

The battered dunes of the hurricane-ravaged shore lay ahead in the macabre gloom of the stormy afternoon. And they weren't going to make it. The twenty-minute flight didn't take much fuel—but they'd lost the tank all too fast.

The engine sputtered.

Kieran looked at Paige where she'd sat, knuckles pale, face tense, since he'd told her they were losing fuel. "It's time."

She didn't have to ask—time for what? She'd gone to the rear of the craft as soon as he'd explained the situation. They'd both already donned life preservers, hoping against hope they wouldn't need them, that the fuel would last. But it had been a futile hope from the beginning.

He could see a town beyond the dunes, not far, and not big. They were somewhere north of Savannah, and that's all he knew. That, and the fact that bodies of water gave him the occasional panic attack—an ironic factor in the hell of his life on Callula Island. A PAX psychiatrist had analyzed it as a manifestation of guilt for not saving Annelie's life. Even though he'd been all of twelve years old when she'd slipped from his desperate grasp and drowned. Head baggage.

"Unlatch your door," he told her. He knew her well enough to see the fear she was trying to hide. "Swim toward shore and don't look back. I'll be right behind you."

The choppy waters below were dangerous, even with life preservers, but they had no choice. He'd brought the helicopter into a low hover using the inertia of the spinning rotor system. They were as close to the beach as they were going to get.

She nodded, and he saw the resilience in her that he'd always admired. "I know you will be," she said. "You're not going to leave me on that beach alone."

There was grim faith in her eyes. She and the PAX psychiatrist were among the few people in the world who knew about the weakness he'd always found embarrassing. She'd always made light of it to him—*even Superman had his Kryptonite.*

She'd had an amazing way of making him feel okay about himself no matter what.

But nothing was okay right now. They both knew they had no idea who or what could be waiting for them, already looking for them. And she had to know as he did that he wasn't going to swim to shore with his computer. There was no turning back now, if there ever had been. He'd stuffed the data disk, the cash, and the gun in his jacket pockets, zipped them in, and prayed any of it would be any good by the time they made it to the beach.

"Hurry," he told her, his throat full. And she turned and pushed out. Sick nausea burned in Kieran's gut. He heard a splash over the wild wind and the still-spinning blades and had to force himself not to think about her chances.

The craft was going down, and fast. He made one

last maneuver, rolling the helicopter on its side. It struck the sea with a loud rush that immediately stopped the blades, and he knew it would sink like a stone. He had seconds to get out.

Clambering up over the passenger seat, he threw himself through the open doorway and into the stormy sea. The ocean cold consumed him in shock for several seconds, then he kicked into a swim, gulping in salty water and spitting as he kept tearing up the sea with his arms. Clothing dragged at him, sodden material pulling him down. A wave tore over his head, and he was under for an awful moment, lost in the hallucinatory world of endless water, before the life vest bounced him back up.

He emerged choking, gasping, looking for Paige. He screamed her name, and the wind tore the sound of his voice away. The post-hurricane swells surged toward the beach, relentless, and he fought to swim with it—mindful of the possibility of also being ripped back out—while searching between breaths for Paige. As long as he thought about Paige, he couldn't panic. That was the rule. Every second lasted forever. Waves kept piling over him, and every time, caught in the power of that heaving water, he had to fight the fear that he wasn't going to come back up. He was going to drown. But he'd fight to the top of the water again and scream for Paige. That was his job, to keep coming up and looking for Paige.

Then a last swell went over his head, took him down again, tossing and scraping him along the sandy, sharp-shelled bottom, leaving him staggering on the ravaged shoreline as the wave sucked backward.

Paige grabbed him as he stumbled to his knees, pulling him up the beach, away from the pounding shoreline. He flopped onto his back, exhaustion leaving him rubbery and trembling. Paige fell beside him. Wind and waves and his heart sounded loud in his ears, and all he could think was—*Paige had made it.*

He turned his head and stared at her. She stared back, hair stuck to her cheeks, clothes soaked. Beautiful and alive.

His ribs hurt, his back hurt, his head hurt— But God, he was *so* okay, because Paige was okay.

Neither of them said anything for a long moment, catching their breath.

Then, "I couldn't see you in the water," he said, and his chest felt so tight as he remembered that fear, finally able to allow it free rein. "Damn waves kept crashing over my head—" He couldn't stop himself from reaching out, touching her face. Then he pulled back before he did something crazy, like kiss her again.

"Me, too," she said softly, her blue eyes shining, liquid. "But I knew you'd make it, Kieran. I knew you'd be here."

That made one of them.

A light rain pecked down. As if they weren't wet enough.

"I'm not invincible, Paige," he said. "And you know it." She needed to get it through her head—he wasn't a hero. In fact, he was just one big, bad, messed-up experiment who was liable to fail her at any turn because his body and soul were on a razor-edge without the containment serum.

"I know how you feel about water," she said, "but things are different now. I figured you could always dog-paddle. Or wolf paddle, in your case."

Kieran stared at her for a long, unblinking moment.

He couldn't remember the last time he'd laughed. He couldn't remember the last time he'd *felt* like laughing. He'd forgotten how damn good it felt to laugh.

And how beautiful Paige looked when she laughed with him.

The rain, their already sopping clothes, their exhausted bodies, and hell, even the ferocious thing inside him didn't matter. And somehow sweet, strong Paige was making him feel as if the thing inside him, taking him over, didn't matter to her, either. That he was okay. Just like she always did.

That thought sobered him.

"We need to get out of here," he said, and pushed to his feet. He held a hand down to Paige, braced himself for the flash of awareness touching her yielded.

She pushed up to her elbows and stared out at the stormy gray ocean. "The helicopter's disappeared," she said then reached up to allow him to draw her to her feet, and she shivered in the cool air as wind whipped over the water toward them.

The beach was deserted, but beyond the dunes, he could see a line of homes, roofs torn, devastated by the high winds. The area would have been evacuated, but people would be returning now.

Something sharp and jagged flashed through her eyes as she gazed out at the sea. "They'll be after us," Paige said.

"With the helicopter sunk, they won't know where to start," he pointed out. He took her hand in grim determination. "One lucky break."

They just needed, oh, about a thousand more of them.

Chapter 7

"Take back that bag of caramels. See if I can afford that."

The very large, very wet woman standing in front of Paige and Kieran in the Dixie Quik Pak watched while the longsuffering convenience store clerk minused out the bag of caramels from her total. A television perched high on the wall ran a news channel reporting on the storm damage up and down the coast.

"Sixteen fifty-four," the clerk said.

The woman eyed the pile of cigarette cartons, candy bags, and beer. "Okay, take back the dark chocolates. Try that."

Clearly she had her priorities all straight. Cigs and beer.

"Did you hear about that helicopter that went down offshore?" a man said behind Kieran.

Paige stiffened and resisted the urge to turn, show any interest in the question. She heard another man behind her respond.

"Nobody'd be flying in this weather," he said.

"A neighbor of mine said she saw a helicopter go down," the first man insisted. "Right offshore. She called it in to the cops."

Great. Paige gave a side glance at Kieran. He held her gaze and said nothing but she could see the ready alert in his posture.

They both looked like drowned rats, standing there in the store dripping onto the floor. Luckily, everyone else looked about the same. It was pouring down rain outside now.

"Fourteen thirty," the clerk said.

"All right!" The heavy woman counted out the cash down to the pennies. She took her loot and headed for the door. She was barefoot, and as she hiked the bag of cigarettes and beer to her chest to dig in her purse for car keys, an expanse of flabby tummy shone in the harsh fluorescent light.

Outside, the afternoon sky hung darkly over the cars splattering up to the parking lot. The convenience store was one of the few businesses they'd found reopened as evacuees returned to the area. They'd walked into the town, squishing in their shoes with every step, feeling like they were walking into a post-apocalyptic world of fallen trees, downed lines, and turned-over cars.

Kieran and Paige set down their supply of overpriced toiletries—toothbrushes, soap, shampoo—along with a few snacks and canned drinks. So close to the beach, the store sold a few handy items geared to tourists—and so they'd picked up some T-shirts as well.

The clerk rang up their purchases and Kieran pulled out a wet wad of cash.

"You don't happen to know of anyone looking to sell a vehicle, do you?" he asked the clerk. "Ours got tackled by a tree in the storm."

The clerk looked up from the greenbacks Kieran was laying out on the counter, separating the stuck-together bills.

"I don't think—"

"My brother's selling his car," the woman with the beer and cigarettes said from the door of the store, hesitating in the opening.

"What's he want for it?" Paige asked as the woman watched Kieran return the remaining cash back to his pocket. Kieran picked up their purchases then followed her to the door.

The men at the counter behind them continued to

bat back and forth the likelihood of anyone really seeing a helicopter go down in the ocean in the aftermath of the hurricane.

"I don't know how much," the woman said. "It's one of them little cars. It's kind of banged up but it runs good. Since his wife's got their fourth one on the way, he's wanting to get something bigger. Want me to give him a call?"

They stepped outside the store. The woman set down the bag and dug a cell phone out of the recesses of her purse. She could barely afford her beer, cigs, and candy habit, but of course she had a cell phone. Paige watched the woman talk for a few minutes, then punch off.

"He'll be up here in a couple minutes," she said.

"Great." Kieran looked at Paige. "See, honey? I told you we'd find something."

Paige felt a little zippy shiver go up her spine that had nothing to do with the gray sky and chilly wind and sopping wet clothes. He'd called her honey. He was faking it, of course. So it shouldn't bug her. He'd called her his wife, too. That had felt stupidly familiar and right for something that was so over. And she thought about that damn goodbye kiss of his, and part of her was still in mourning, but another part felt only anger. How could he just kiss her goodbye like that?

She looked at Kieran, standing there in his shirt torn from the rough shore, and for a fleeting, dangerous moment she wished all the pain of their past didn't stand between them. She wanted to feel his arms around her again, absorb his heat. Instead, she rubbed her hands up and down her arms, trying to ward off the chill of her damp clothes and the overcast sky. But the exertion did nothing to take away the surge of emotion.

The next hours, days, however long before he left her, really would be goodbye, and she knew she didn't want it to end this way, with this chasm of pain aching between them. It just felt wrong, and she didn't know how to make it right.

She crossed her arms now and sat on the curb beneath the overhang of the store. The woman tore open a package of cigarettes, lit up, and babbled on about her brood of nieces and nephews while Paige tried to block out the torment of her own thoughts. She drew her knees to her chest and tugged them tight.

The guy was taking forever to get to the store. And they needed to get the heck out of Dodge, especially since they knew someone had reported a helicopter going down in the area. She glanced up to where Kieran stood and could tell by the set of his hard jaw that he was getting antsy, too. He began to pace, his strides clipped and restless as he watched the street.

A police cruiser rolled down the road in front of the convenience store, turned into the lot. Nerves knotted Paige's stomach as two officers got out. Any chance the traitor in PAX had dummied up a bulletin on her and Kieran and sent it out to agencies along the coast? Anything was possible. She sat dead still as they walked past them without a glance and went into the store. She watched Kieran's piercing, haunted gaze follow them then return to her, lock for one taut beat before turning away.

"You two got any kids?" the woman asked Kieran, stubbing her smoke out.

Kieran's gaze pinned Paige's again, then he glanced away. "No," he said.

Paige's heart squeezed. They'd never really talked about kids. Paige had brought it up a few times, but Kieran had resisted even discussing it. Later, he always said. Later never came. Kieran had been a master at sidestepping conversations of any substance.

She'd refused to see it in those days. Refused to accept that Kieran wasn't ready, might never be ready, and that she couldn't change anything.

She'd seen what she wanted to see.

"There he is," the woman said suddenly. She waved at the small red Gremlin pulling into the lot. Her brother parked next to the police cruiser.

She wasn't kidding about the car being banged up. It looked like it had had been driven through a war zone in the twenty-something years since the vehicle had been manufactured.

A stringy-haired man got out and came toward them. He looked like he was maybe twenty-five, and his oh-so-pregnant and pretty wife looked about twelve, but she couldn't be, not with the three wet and whiny little kids that piled out of the back.

"What's wrong with it?" Kieran probed.

"Well, it's dropping oil," the guy told him. "But you can go a couple hundred miles before you have to fill it up. And you can't roll down the driver's side window, but you can roll down the passenger's side, which is good because you can't open the door from the inside—"

"It runs," the wife said, giving her husband a hard look. "It's a classic."

Only if a classic could be defined as a rolling pile of junk.

"Okay, how much?" Kieran asked, impatient.

The wife's eyes narrowed, proving she really wasn't twelve if the kids hadn't. She didn't give her husband time to answer.

"Three hundred."

Kieran counted out three wet bills.

"I got the paperwork here," the guy said, yanking it from his back pocket.

Kieran exchanged the cash for the key and the papers. Paige scooted into the passenger seat. Kieran got in and jammed the key in the ignition, tossing the paperwork in the backseat. The Gremlin shook and groaned as they pulled out of the lot just as the cops came out with mega-size drink cups.

Tires splashed as he accelerated down the water-logged road. He fiddled around and hit on the head-lights as dark, closed businesses slid by outside the car windows. They reached the last stoplight out of town. Signs with cities and mileage markers pointed in several directions. Paige passed Kieran a canned drink and a bag of chips while they waited for the light to turn.

"Nineteen-eighty called," she said. "They want their car back."

Kieran glanced at her, and she saw the bleary, bloodshot fatigue in those dark, depthless eyes of his. How long since he'd slept? He looked like it could have been weeks. He'd told her he wasn't invincible, but he seemed bound and determined to act as if he was. He was stretching the limits of his endurance, and a sharp concern for him pulled at her chest.

"Too bad we can't go back with it," he said finally.

Paige swallowed tightly. Time travel. Now that would be a handy power right about now. PAX needed to work on that one.

The light turned from red to green.

Kieran gazed straight ahead. The car didn't move. His eyes were fierce on the signal lights. Something in that unflinching stare unnerved her.

Her stomach twisted. "Are you all right?" she asked.

He looked at her. "I'm fine." He didn't look fine. He looked haggard and drawn. He was in pain, she realized. But he wouldn't mention it, not to her.

"The light's green," she said. "Let's go."

He stared back at the light, blinked, and put the car in gear. But she didn't feel any better. She felt so much worse, and she didn't even know why.

They hit I-95 North for an hour, pulling over for gas and oil after thirty minutes. They'd crossed the South Carolina line, and Kieran registered that they weren't far from where he'd grown up. The familiarity of the Lowcountry palmetto forests tugged at something deep and lost inside him. At the gas station, Kieran stuck a quarter in the phone and punched in Dub's cell number. The air hung heavy around them, thick with the recent storm. Wind rustled in the trees behind the station. The rain had slowed to a drizzle.

He'd been experiencing periodic pain since they'd left the coastal town. The frequency of the pain was what worried him the most. The increasing rate of the tight, prickling bouts reminded him that time was running out. What if the next time he shifted, he couldn't come back? That dread was always with him, but even more so now. It was one of several reasons he prayed to God he wouldn't shift again while he was with Paige.

A few other cars were parked at the pumps. Everything seemed normal. No one seemed to be following them.

"Dub?"

There was silence for a second. "Kieran? You're alive." He heard Dub take a shaking breath. "Damn it, you scared the living crap out of me. Where are you? How the hell are you at a phone?" He drew in another sharp breath that made it all the way through the phone lines. "You know I told Paige where you were. I'm sorry, man—"

"Forget it. Has anyone been there? Anyone been bothering you?" All along it had killed him, worrying that Dub would be hurt because of him. And now— He didn't know what could happen now. He wanted Dub someplace safe till this thing blew over. Safe with Paige.

"No. I mean, nobody lately. They were swarming all over me in the beginning, till they gave up and believed me that I didn't know where you were. But yesterday, there was this one guy, and *he* was scared of *me,* I swear," Dub said. "Said his name was Brian something. *Where are you?*" he repeated.

Kieran's stomach dropped. He ignored Dub's question. "Brian Kaplan?" His gaze jerked to Paige. "He came to your house?"

Dub lived more often than not on his boat anchored off the busy fishing wharfs in Savannah. His girlfriend lived in a mobile home park on the edge of the city, but mostly, Dub was kicked out. His not-so-legal sidelines were a source of conflict.

"No, he came to Blind Bob's," he said, naming a downtown bar he frequented. "He must have followed me there, or asked someone."

"What'd he want?" Kieran's blood churned. All this time, and now Brian had turned up. What did that mean?

"He just gave me a number, that's all. Hang on. Gotta find it."

Kieran motioned to Paige that he needed something to write with. She patted the pockets of her jacket, looking for her pen, which she apparently realized was long gone. She ran back to the car.

She came back and handed him a crayon. He quirked his brow.

"What do you want?" she said. "That's all I could find. If you don't like that color, there's a whole box in the back seat on the floorboard."

As if he even knew what color it was. It was red or green, he knew that, but those colors were impossible for him to differentiate in his vision anymore.

"Here it is," Dub said. He reeled off a number. Kieran jotted it down on a scrap of paper he'd torn from the phone book attached to the booth.

"What'd he look like?" Kieran wasn't assuming the mysterious person who'd come to see Dub was really Brian, not yet.

"Little guy," Dub said. "Like, five foot six, maybe. Light hair. Round glasses. He was downing shooters like there was no tomorrow. Shaky. Had one of those accents, you know, like Rocky. Except he sure as hell didn't look like Rocky."

Close enough. Brian was from Philly.

"Did he say anything?"

"No," Dub answered. "Just that he wanted to get hold of you. I told him I had no idea how to get in touch with you, but he insisted on leaving his number anyway."

"Are you home now?"

"No, I headed out when the hurricane hit. I'm about to head back."

"Don't go back, Dub," Kieran said then. "I can't explain, but it's getting hot. I had to leave the island. Just trust me on this."

"I got a deal going down—"

Dub *always* had a deal going down. Usually, an illegal one.

"I don't want you to die, Dub."

"Are you trying to scare me?"

"Yes." But he knew Dub didn't scare easily and it would take more. Dub might not do this for himself, but he'd do it for Paige. He glanced at her and held his hand over the phone for a second. "Check inside. We need a map." Paige went into the building then he said to Dub, "I don't want anything to happen to

Paige, either, and I'm counting on you. Do you know if Harry ever goes to the cabin anymore?" The old family summer place near the Shenandoah River had been an occasional oasis of normalcy from Kieran's strung-out home life when Dub's parents would take him and Annelie with them on their vacations. It was owned by a second cousin now.

Kieran hadn't been back there since Annelie died.

"Harry's on a sabbattical, doing some kind of research in South America. Some kind of Amazon forest thing. He sent me a postcard a couple months back."

"Great." He didn't want Harry in the way. It was bad enough that Paige and Dub were both in danger because of him. The last thing he wanted to do was put anyone else in the cross-fire.

"Go to the cabin," he told Dub. "If you have the slightest idea you're being followed, turn back." Dub had been ditching authorities for most of his teenage and adult life, so he had as good a chance as anyone of watching his back. "I'll meet you there tomorrow night. And I'm leaving Paige there."

Now he just had to get Paige to the cabin. The two people he cared most about in the world would be safe, and he would do what he had to do.

Paige returned with the map as he hung up the phone. Her eyes were steady and cool, collected. She was scared under all that poise, he could see it. But she was so determined to be strong. And she was. She was a PAX agent, and a damn good one, even though he'd never wished more than he did now that she'd never been one.

Had he ever told her he was proud of her? Had he ever taken the time to even think about it during their marriage? He wasn't sure. He was sure he'd spent a lot of time thinking about the most precious person on the planet riding around beneath the waves in an experimental MUV, Marine Underwater Vehicle, without him. She'd always return from research trips thrilled, and he would be anything but.

Even as he'd recognized his overprotectiveness, he hadn't been able to control it. Or maybe he'd decided not to because the battles he'd created kept him from having to admit how much he needed Paige. The observation did nothing to make him feel better.

"You're a damn fine PAX agent, Paige," he said softly. "If I never told you that before, I want you to know now." God, those words sounded empty, not good enough, but in her shiny eyes he saw her gaze wobble just a bit.

And he had a bad, bad feeling that if he needed to push her away now, he'd just made a mistake. He felt his own hard edges splintering at the softness in her eyes and he couldn't afford that weakness. Paige couldn't afford that weakness in him. He'd let her down before, and he would not let her down now.

Even if it killed him.

Thank God she didn't say anything in response, just picked up another quarter from the pile he'd laid on the ledge under the pay phone. "Call Brian."

Chapter 8

Another coin clattered into the phone slot. Paige watched Kieran punch in the numbers from the scrap of paper then he stuffed the scrap in his back pocket. The drizzle picked up, rain slapping the pavement around them. Wind rustled in the tree. The chilly aftermath of Hurricane Bernadette seemed to follow them.

She just hoped no one else was.

Kieran's mouth looked grim. Paige was wet and cold and tired, and she knew he had to be, too.

She shivered under the ominous, drenching sky and wondered when either of them would get a chance to rest.

"Brian? Is that you?"

Her insides clenched as she watched the sharp measuring in Kieran's eyes. He didn't know who to trust, and neither did she. Brian had disappeared not long after Kieran had gone. Now, he was back, trying to get in touch with Kieran. Why?

"It's me, Kieran."

Leaning in, she tried to make out the voice on the phone.

"Where you have been all this time?" Brian asked. His voice was low, urgent, and Paige had a hard time picking up all his words. The fact that Brian's cell phone kept cutting out didn't help. "If only I could have found you. I know you didn't do it, Holt. But I was alone."

"Do you have some kind of evidence? Do you know who destroyed the lab, killed Phil?" Kieran peppered the questions at Brian.

"It's big, Kieran. They've killed for it already. And I don't mean Phil."

"Who's they?"

Brian's voice went even lower. He was almost whispering now. "They've already tried to kill me. That's why I left PAX. But I was wrong. They came after me. There's only one way out. I have to prove what happened. It's the only way out for any of us."

Kieran's body looked completely rigid. *"Tell me what you know."*

"I'm getting on a plane in an hour. I know where to get the proof. Call me at this number tomorrow night." He said something else that was cut off by static. "If I'm not there—" static broke in again "—Masterson."

"What about Shay Masterson?" Kieran demanded. "Where will I meet you?"

"—airport," Brian said. "If I don't make it— Tell Talia—bank." More static.

"What did he say?" she demanded when Kieran put the phone down. "Did you get that?" The rain kept coming down, but she didn't care. He ignored her, picked the phone up, stuck another coin in and jabbed Brian's number in again, then swore and slammed it down.

"He's not picking up." His look was unbelievable frustration.

"We'll try again later."

They both knew later wasn't good enough.

"It's pouring," Kieran said then. "Get in the car. I'll be right there. I need to make one more call. Old friend of mine."

Paige didn't move. "Who are you calling?"

Kieran's expression took on an even darker tension. "This is an old friend from juvy. He's got a talent I could use. This isn't exactly legal, Paige. You don't need to know about it."

She still didn't go back to the car. Kieran cast another irritated look at her and stuck another coin in the phone.

Too bad. She wasn't going anywhere, rain or no rain. She wasn't surprised when he punched in an old number from memory. His talented mind was what had drawn PAX's attention in the beginning. He had an almost photographic memory.

"Scott? Kieran Holt. How are you doing these days?" Kieran tapped his finger against the phone booth for a few impatient moments of small talk. "Look, I need you to do something for me. I need you to hack into some D.C. bank records." He gave Scott the names of the task force members, plus Talia's, Vinn's, and Brian's.

Paige waited till he put the phone down. "What makes you think he can do that?"

"I know he can." Kieran took her arm and pulled her to the car. "Why do you think he was in juvy?" He yanked the passenger side open and Paige slid inside.

He came around to the driver's side and stabbed the key into the ignition. The cranky Gremlin rattled to life. They pulled out of the gas station lot with rain sluicing down the car's glass. Kieran hit the lights and the windshield wipers.

The wiper blades slap-slapped.

"What I want to know is how Brian would know anything about anyone's bank records," Kieran said.

"He dated a girl who worked at a bank, remember?" Paige said.

Kieran thought about that for a minute. "Do you remember her name?"

Paige shook her head. "Maybe we could track her down."

Kieran's mouth set grimly. "I don't have time to track her down. If there's something to find, Scott will find it," he said. "There's got to be cash involved here. Big cash."

"Where does Brian want to meet?"

"You don't need to know," Kieran told her, his gaze intent on his driving. He headed up the on-ramp to the interstate. "He wants to meet with *me,* Paige. Not *you.* You'll be long gone by then."

Paige's spine stiffened. "You aren't going to meet Brian without me."

Kieran gave a violent flick of the Gremlin's turn signal as he got ready to negotiate the merge into interstate traffic. "This is dangerous, Paige. It could be a trap."

Paige waved his words away. "I don't care. Look," she added when Kieran's face remained impassive, "Brian left PAX." Suspecting Brian seemed like a stretch, but Kieran had thrown his name in to Scott along with all the others.

"Right," Kieran ground out. "He left PAX. Why?" He cut her a hard look, then turned back to focus on the rain-slick road. "We can't trust anyone, Paige. When are you going to get that straight?"

A flash of anger tugged at her gut. "I've got it straight, Kieran," she said bitterly. "Maybe what *you* don't have straight is that you don't have to protect me. I'm a big girl. I'm a PAX agent, just like you. You just got through telling me what a great one I am, too. Guess you didn't really mean that."

Kieran swore, and yanked the wheel, pulling the Gremlin sharply to the left and sliding to a sharp stop on the gravelly side of the road. Paige's heart picked up its pace.

The engine ran, stumbling every few seconds as if it were gasping for air. Cars swished by, throwing up water on the side windows.

Then Kieran spoke, his voice dark and strained. "Dammit, Paige, how many times do I have to tell you that I don't want you hurt?"

She tipped her chin, refusing to acknowledge that his concern mattered to her in any way other than as an annoyance. "How many times do I have to tell you that I don't need your protection? We're in this together whether you like it or not."

She knew he was bound and determined to ditch her and she was just as bound and determined that she wouldn't be ditched. So far, he hadn't even trusted her enough to tell her where and when he was leaving her.

"What exactly do you intend to do? Tie me up? Lock me in a car trunk? Do I get to know where we're headed or is that on a need-to-know basis?" As in, he didn't think she needed to know.

"This is a limited partnership, Paige." He clipped the words out at her. Frustration lit his dark eyes. "It ends just as soon as I can leave you in the cabin at Buck's Run with Dub."

Now she knew. He was taking her to the mountain cabin at Buck's Run where he'd spent his boyhood summers. Dropping her off with Dub like a child at day care. Then he'd disappear, head back to PAX without her to save the world all by himself.

He didn't need her.

"Right. Limited partnership." Hurt closed her throat. "Kind of like, oh, *our marriage,* come to think of it."

Her sarcastic words hovered in the taut air between them.

"You're right," Kieran said, his voice surprisingly quiet, a thread of pain she recognized too well sliding just beneath the surface. "I was a bastard. I admit it. I wasn't a good husband, and you deserved better. You deserve better now, and I'm going to be damned if you get yourself killed before you get the chance."

She didn't know what to say to that. She felt as if he'd taken the wind out of her sails. Yes, he'd been a difficult man to live with.... Distant, withdrawn, secretive. But he'd been a fantastic husband, too. He'd made her laugh, made her cry, made her heart soar when he smiled. They'd been each other's family when neither of them had much of one.

When he was good, he was very, very good, and when he was bad... The words bubbled up in her mind and she didn't know whether to laugh or cry.

"If you're going to meet Brian, I'm going with you," she said finally. She still couldn't respond to his comment about what kind of husband he'd been. Her heart was too tangled up on that one to attempt expressing any feelings at all, especially to the one man responsible for all her messed-up emotions. "He could have crucial information," she insisted. "Information that could save your life and save PAX."

"If he has important information that could save PAX, why isn't he taking it to PAX?"

Paige's pulse kicked up. "I don't know. That's what we need to find out."

The taut line of his mouth didn't change, and the fact was, she could protest all she wanted. He had his own plans and she wasn't part of them.

Kieran craned his head back to check the lane before moving back onto the interstate. Paige flicked the radio knob, relieved to find the old car's sound system worked. Scratchy jazz filled the uncomfortable air between her and the man she was still married to. She turned the dial till she found a radio station she liked then slid the volume knob to a level that would serve to discourage further conversation.

Not that Kieran looked eager to talk. He had his gaze firmly fixed on the wet road ahead. Whatever feelings he'd experienced while they'd been parked at the side of the interstate, he'd firmly tucked them back in place. He was way too good at that trick.

So why, with all that hurt and residual anger simmering beneath the surface, did just looking at him still yield an unwanted jolt of sexual attraction? Sure, sex had been good between them. Kieran was a handsome man, and Paige was a passionate woman. Just observing the way his muscular frame filled out the damp shirt he wore surfaced memories of how it would feel to touch the bare shoulders and biceps beneath that thin material.

He'd grown leaner in his years on Callula Island, but he hadn't lost muscle mass. Rather, he was more athletic than before, more appealing, more masculine. There was something raw and real about him now, a power honed by nature not the gym. Rebellious desire curled to life inside her.

Her palms were sweating, her stomach muscles dancing. Oh, yeah, she could find herself practically drooling over him, too, if she didn't watch out. How stupid was that? It was one thing to feel a little tug of bittersweet memory when he kissed her, but to let herself keep thinking about it....

Okay, that had been more than a little tug, more than a memory, she'd felt those two times they'd kissed on Callula Island.

But now— She had no business on God's green earth thinking about him that way now.

She forced herself to stare out the passenger-side window. She was angry with him, had been angry with him for two years, and no matter what his reasoning, he'd been wrong to leave her the way he had two years ago. She'd be nuts, certifiable, if she gave him another chance to hurt her, even if he wanted to give her that chance.

Suddenly, she touched the inside pocket of her jacket. The folded, damp divorce document was still there. All she had to do was hand the paper over to her lawyer and she would no longer be Mrs. Kieran Holt. It was something she should have done two years ago, but had somehow been unable to bring herself to do.

She'd tried, a couple of times. Both times, she'd sat there in the parking lot of the law office, her breath lodged in her throat, her stomach tight with panic. And she'd driven away without going inside.

After Kieran had disappeared, she'd spent a month on involuntary leave from PAX, unable to return to work until she'd been cleared of any involvement by the investigation. She'd spent way too much time sitting around, depressed, in front of afternoon TV pop psychologists. She could just hear Dr. Phil now....

So you thought you could change him when you married him, hmm? How's that working for you?

Her heart smarted at the obvious answer. Not too good. Not too good at all.

Then she remembered that a divorce might be completely unnecessary. Long before she made it back to her attorney's office, Kieran might be dead.

Kieran left the interstate and hit a state highway heading north. The interstates worried him. He was paranoid, and he had reason. The downed helicopter had been reported back where they'd come ashore. He couldn't stop someone from tracking them, but he could make it harder. If they'd asked enough questions in that small coastal town outside of Savannah, they could be looking for the Gremlin already.

As they drove past a midsize town, a strip of hotels appeared on the outskirts. It was getting dark, and he was exhausted and starving. A dazzling-to-Kieran's-deprived-eyes array of fast-food restaurants lined the road. His mouth watered immediately.

He pulled in to the first one and asked Paige what she wanted. He ordered two burgers with everything for himself, and two extra-large fries. He might be too tired to eat them, but he wanted them. Just smelling the aromas wafting out through the drive-up window was killing him. He hadn't had food like this in two years.

"Big Mac attack?" Paige asked.

There was a delightful, teasing quirk to her lips that made it impossible for him to not think about the freaking stupid move he'd made before they left the cave. Her mouth had been so soft—

"Something like that," he said briefly and looked back at the drive-up window because he didn't trust himself to look at Paige right then. Looking at Paige made him think about what else he hadn't had in two years. And they were heading for a hotel.

It'd be a hell of a lot safer for his libido to get two rooms. But they had a limited cash supply, not to mention, if someone tracked them down— He didn't want Paige in a hotel room alone.

Luckily, he was way too tired for temptation to be a serious threat. Not that exhaustion was keeping his rampant imagination from going wild thinking about Paige stretched out on a hotel bed, all silky skin and round breasts and long, long legs—

So what if even tired as all get out, he could remember all too well how it felt to push himself inside her, her arms clinging to him, her head thrown sexily back? It wasn't going to happen.

He paid for the food and passed the delicious-smelling bags to Paige, then pulled out of the fast-food lot directly into the first hotel, parking in the rear. They checked in and paid in cash.

Their fifth floor room was the last one on an interior corridor, with two double beds and cable TV. There was a balcony overlooking a swimming pool he could just make out in the clouded night. They had no luggage but their little stash of convenience store purchases and their fast-food bags.

Kieran walked in after Paige. He checked the lock on the sliding glass doors then pulled the drapes shut before he sat down on one of the upholstered chairs by a table. She set out the food and he wolfed down every last bite of his own.

"This must be weird for you," she said, watching him. She was eating in dainty bites, hungry but not like an animal. Like him. "People come back from reality TV shows where they've stayed on deserted islands for a month and are crazy for all the creature comforts. It's been two years for you."

"I didn't miss much," he said. Then damn, he saw the spear of something dark in her eyes and he knew he'd screwed up.

He didn't want to hurt her, and it seemed as if that's all he did. He'd just wanted to push her away at first, for her own good. Now—

Nothing had changed since she'd landed on Callula Island, and yet it had at the same time. But he didn't know what to say to make it better.

"I mean, I learned to block out the things I was missing," he said quietly. "I didn't let myself think that way."

She nodded in a brittle kind of way. "Sure. I understand."

He wasn't hungry anymore. And he had no idea what to say to make Paige not hurt.

"Why don't you take the shower first," she suggested stiffly, wadding the fast-food wrappers from her meal in her fist. "I'm going to check the news."

She sat at the end of one of the beds and punched the TV remote.

He knew she didn't expect to learn anything relating to their situation. That sort of information didn't make it to the media. She was just done talking, and that was a good thing, he reminded himself. All he should be thinking about was getting back to Washington, getting the serum, and taking down the traitor. Exhaustion pulled at him as he entered the bathroom.

The shower was like some kind of nirvana experience. He could have slept standing under that hot fall of blessed water, but he remembered he had to save some hot water for Paige.

She took her turn when he came out. He heard the door click behind her and he tried not to see her in his mind, under the water, naked…

He went to the far bed, near the window, and crashed on it. He'd forgotten how good beds felt. He felt as if he was floating on the incredible mattress, and he let himself shut his eyes, just feel the soft, long-lost comfort of clean sheets and warm blankets. The water stopped, and after a few minutes, he heard Paige come out of the bathroom.

Was she naked?

No, that was crazy. Like she'd come gliding out of the shower to him all bare and ready. But he kept his eyes closed because it was a nice thought and he wanted to hold on to it.

Reality was overrated.

Fantasy… That was much better. In his fantasies, Paige was naked.

He felt her sit down on the bed near him. She smelled soooo good. Like home.

"I remember now," he sighed. "I missed mattresses."

"I bet you did." She touched his shoulders, his back, massaging at the sore muscles through the fresh T-shirt he'd donned. Her fingers did a slow, sensual dance across his shoulders, kneading, rubbing. It felt too good.

God, what was she doing? And he remembered how much he'd missed her, too. The feeling keened through him, so long denied.

It would be too dangerous an admission to make out loud in that moment. Especially while he was still seeing her naked.

She was just being nice, that's all. Paige was a nice person. *And he was not.*

"I shouldn't sleep," he said, but his heavy lids

didn't want to lift. He needed to stay awake—what if someone tracked them here somehow? He expected them to be looking for him. They'd eluded any pursuers, but for how long?

Sleep dragged on his weary body despite his thoughts.

What if he dreamed? What if he frightened Paige?

He had learned to dread dreams. In some ways, they were worse than actual physical shifts. He remembered the dream shifts.

"Let go," she said softly. "You're not going to be any good tomorrow without sleep."

He could smell the aroma of burgers and fries still lingering in the air. He could smell Paige, sweetly scrubbed with soap and shampoo.

"Let go," she whispered again, and it was the last thing he remembered before he dropped into a deep sleep.

He woke to his own personal version of hell.

Chapter 9

He was back in the dark, tangled jungle of Callula Island.

The animal self inside simmered, rose, separating from him, leaving both of them poised for flight in the thick, dangerous woods, and yet neither could run. The wolf was terrified of him, and he was terrified of the wolf.

Then the animal leaped at him, ripped open his shoulder. Kieran felt the pain burn into him and yet he couldn't move. He couldn't run from the wolf. And then the wolf was him, they were one being, and formless beasts snarled from the woods. He ran on all fours, dripping blood from both his shoulder and his mouth. He came to a cliff—and there was no way out. No way but down, down, into the depthless water below. Then Annelie appeared, wraithlike, from the woods, running toward him even as the beasts arrived.

The faces of the beasts morphed from formless to real—Julius Kelley, Brigitte Perry, Kent Oberman, Talia Regan, Shay Masterson, and back again to blurred, snarling heads with fangs. Now it wasn't Annelie anymore, it was Paige and she was between him and the beasts. He screamed her name and lunged, fighting.

"Stop!"

He heard the word from somewhere outside himself, but the world of words had no meaning. He existed in pure awareness. He knew something wrapped around his waist, trying to contain him, and with all his might, he fought it, fought for Paige. He hit something hard and pain slammed him.

Then the voice came again. "Kieran, no!"

His name snapped at his mind, and he saw the eyes desperately pleading with him. Paige's beautiful, haunted eyes.

He pushed away from her, realizing then that he was on the floor of the hotel room beside the bed, and he'd hit the chair with his back. He tried to stand, still not able to speak, but walking on two feet was impossible. He stumbled and she caught him, held him up, pulled him back onto the bed. He crashed onto his back, and she sat beside him, her arm wrapped across his middle as if she feared he wouldn't stay.

"My God, I thought you were going to hurt yourself," she whispered starkly. "It was like you were in some kind of fight!"

He choked in air in rough breaths. His heart thundered hard against the wall of his chest. The beating hooves of the stampeding chase reverberated in his mind. He looked at Paige, and she stared down at him with huge eyes, her aching face pale in the flickering light from the television she must have left on after he'd gone to sleep. His gaze swung around the hotel room as he struggled to orient himself. The numbers on the digital clock read-out by the bed said 3:00 a.m. He pushed onto his elbows, sitting up against the pillow.

"Did I hurt you?" he asked, fumbling to form words, his speech slow, slurred.

"No, of course not," she said. "I was afraid you were going to hurt yourself! I heard you yelling, and I woke up—you leaped off the bed and then you fell. And it was like you were struggling with someone or something."

The nightmare visions of those morphing heads, human and beast all at once, stung his mind.

"I have dream shifts," he said. "They're real. Very real." He closed his eyes as he pressed a shaking hand to his forehead. His pulse hummed as he worked to slow his breathing. He felt the wolf self inside him shrinking, retreating, but not quickly enough. He would have done anything if he could have willed it away faster. The pain of looking into Paige's eyes so close to a shift nearly killed him.

He could lie to Paige, and he could lie to himself, about his real feelings for her, but he couldn't lie to his animal self. His wolf side lived on a sharp edge of truth.

"I'm sorry that I frightened you," he said roughly, rubbing his eyes, forcing himself to look at her again and steeling the human will inside him as he did. "I ruined your sleep. I'll be fine now." Thank God the words were starting to form easier on his lips.

She didn't say anything for a long beat. "You don't have to pretend with me," she said, and there was an angry strain in her voice. "You don't have to say you're okay when you're not."

"It's nothing you need to know, Paige." His nightmare shifts were a burden she didn't deserve. And she was carrying enough hell on her shoulders for what she already knew.

She rose abruptly, strode across the room then strode back, arms fisted at her hips. She was wearing that damn beach T-shirt that barely scraped her hips. Sparks flashed in her furious eyes.

"Yes, I do need to know! Stop making decisions for me. Stop protecting me. Stop shutting me out. I do still care about you, you know!"

"Why?"

The question dropped in the room like a bomb to Kieran's ears. He couldn't take it back. He didn't want to take it back. The honesty of his animal self was too strong.

Then to his total misery, he saw tears in Paige's eyes. All the anger left her shoulders, and her arms wrapped around herself.

"You know what?" she whispered thickly. "If you'd ever understood the answer to that question, you wouldn't have left two years ago without me."

Kieran felt like she'd punched him in the gut. He couldn't give Paige what she wanted, needed. He'd never been able to in the past, and he couldn't now. She had this indomitable spirit that had both drawn him and scared him at the same time. He'd never let her get too close even during their marriage. And it was too late for anything to change now.

"I didn't want you to be hurt," he said past the ball of emotion in his throat. "I wanted to spare you any more pain than necessary. It was bad enough that PAX thought I was a traitor. Bad enough that I'd been contaminated with the serum. I knew it was out of control, and that there was no telling what would happen to me. I wanted to cut short the suffering for you." It had made sense at the time. It made sense now.

And yet looking in Paige's ravaged eyes, he knew it had still been wrong. And maybe he was yet too close to the shift to keep lying to himself that he'd only been sparing *her* pain.

He'd been sparing *himself* the pain of facing her. The pain he felt right now. The pain of knowing that what he and Paige had was over.

"I guess I should be thanking you then," she said with sarcasm laced in her thin, strained voice, "for doing me such a nice favor."

"No, you shouldn't be thanking me," he ground out. "You should be running away from me as fast as you can, because if you stick with me, I'm probably going to hurt you some more. That's what people do, Paige. They hurt each other."

The bitterness of his own words burned bile in his throat and he felt sick. He'd never said anything like it out loud before, and he realized the shattering bleakness of it as he did. And he didn't like how that bleakness looked on Paige.

The fragile darkness in her night-sea eyes stabbed him deeper than anything else because for the first time ever, he saw that indomitable spirit in her falter. She'd lived through more foster homes than she could count without losing hope, and he didn't want marriage to him to be the straw that broke her.

He burst off the bed, driven to take back his own darkness from her despite the risk. Her eyes widened as he reached her, and before he could let his own fear stop him, he took her face in his hands.

"Whatever you do, don't listen to me. Forget I ever said that. I want something better for you than what I have."

There was just the slightest wobble in her voice when she replied into the still, dark room. "Why can't you want it for you, too?"

He had. God knew he had, for that magic moment in time when they'd been married. But that ship had sailed a long time ago.

"I don't have much of a future," he managed without his voice breaking. "Don't you get it yet? I don't know if the scrum will work even if I get my hands on it. I don't know if I'm going to make it, no matter what happens. The shifts are getting harder to control. I have steady pain, and my vision is changing. I can't see in human colors anymore. You know that stoplight? I couldn't see when it turned, Paige. I can't tell the difference between red and green anymore. For all I know, the next time I shift, I might not come back."

The look on her face hurt, and he would have turned, would have blocked out the sight of her beautiful, agonized eyes, but she wouldn't let him. She grabbed his arm and pulled him back.

"Then you have *now,*" she whispered. "You have right here, right now."

"Paige, the best thing I can do for you right now is get as far away from you as—"

"Stop deciding what's best for me."

She stepped into the already too narrow gap between them. No more gap.

"I can't handle being this close to you," he told her desperately. All the intense, relentless feelings from the past twenty-four hours, the past two years, surged into a tornado inside him. Despair and grief and need. He was living on a fine edge of control, and it was getting finer all the time.

"Too bad," she said. "Handle it."

And she was so damn close, so tough and proud and unbearably once his. But she was no memory now, she was right here in front of him. He could feel the length of her pressed up to the length of him. He was dying with longing for her.

That fine edge he was living on was crumbling beneath his feet.

Her face was tilted up to him, her mouth near enough to claim. "Tell me what you feel, what you want. I dare you to tell me the truth for once. Is just kissing me goodbye enough, Kieran?"

Rain and wind slapped against the balcony doors.

Maybe it was the fact that she'd called what they were about to do a goodbye. Maybe that made it just safe enough for both of them. He had no doubt that by tomorrow he wouldn't look back on this and think it had been safe at all.

But tonight, it didn't matter.

Kieran kissed her. He *had* to kiss her, or die right then and there from the roiling tumult of guilt and heartache inside his chest. She matched his desperate need kiss for kiss, a broken sob in her throat, clinging to him as if she'd never let go. And God, he prayed she wouldn't let go.

He pulled her backward, and they fell onto the bed together. She straddled over him and his arms streaked down her body, felt the ride of her T-shirt on her hips and the flimsy protection of her sheer panties.

This was so wrong. He knew it, yet he was way beyond stopping. He'd needed her, longed for her, and the way she was kissing him told him she'd needed him and longed for him, too. That revelation alone sent him that much further over the crumbling edge he'd already lost sight of, and there was no way he was going to be the strong one now, the one who would stop this from happening. Her hands were taking stock of his body, relearning every hard plane and muscle even as she kept kissing him like she couldn't get enough.

The world outside, their fractured past and murky future, held no meaning. Then she tore away from him just long enough to grasp the hem of her T-shirt and rip it over her head. Now he wasn't just dying, he'd died. In the flickering light, she stared down at him, bare-breasted and so beautiful, and he could hear nothing but the thunder of his heart.

She slid back onto the bed with him, all scent and shadows and the sweetest of memories. Heat and desire, long denied, shot through him. He had to touch her again, feel her. On a low moan, he pulled her against him, closing his mouth over hers again.

Her fingers tangled in his hair as his hands relived paths not forgotten down her shoulders, her back, her bottom. His body, his heart, jolted at the sensation of erotic memory.

She trembled against him and made a throaty little moan against his mouth and the sound of it drove him wild. He could feel the points of her breasts pressed against his chest through his T-shirt, and the tightness of her thighs around his hips. He swept his hold to the tender curve of her rear and rolled her onto her back beside him. In a quick motion, he tore off his shirt, and came back to crush his mouth to hers again. They were skin to skin now, and it was breathtaking, fantastic, and out of this world wonderful.

God, he'd missed her *so* much.

Then her hands were skimming his shoulders, his back, and reaching between them to touch the hot core of his longing. He felt her desperate hands at the waistband of his shorts, tugging hungrily. He reached down, rolled away long enough to wrestle them off, and when he returned, she circled that hot need with her fingers and it was all he could do not to groan. He reached for her, and found her ready, aching, pressing herself against his hand. She'd never been shy when it came to sex, and her passion equaled his.

In the silvery flicker of the television, she looked ethereal and he could almost believe he was caught in another dream, only this one could never end and he'd be deliriously happy. The unabashed desire in her eager blue-midnight eyes kicked his pulse further into warp speed overdrive. He explored her slick need, and nearly laughed aloud at her own sharp intake of air then he watched her fall apart before his eyes. He wanted to eat her up, swallow her whole, inhale her, but he wanted so desperately to make this last.

She was more impatient. She pulled him over her and arched against him, clinging to his shoulders and demanding more.

"Now, Kieran," she whispered thickly. "I want you, inside, now."

He could have exploded right there. And he was so lost, that if she hadn't breathed his name, he might not have even remembered it. She let out a long husky sigh as he plunged into her, then closed her eyes. On her face, he saw the flashes of delirious pleasure as she lost herself, too. He began to move with excruciating slowness, willing himself to draw out this perfect moment as he kissed her mouth, her eyes, her neck, and she arched beneath him, her fingernails digging into his back, demanding more. She met each thrust with wild abandon, out of control and exciting him to a feverish tempo. His blood pumped, and he felt her softly shudder and melt even as her teeth dug into his shoulder.

With torturous restraint, he slowed down, but she would have none of it.

"Don't stop," she breathed, and gripped his buttocks in her hands and arched against him again, entreating more, quickening the rhythm. She threw her head back in sheer, blind exhilaration and he leaned down to catch her delectable nipples in his mouth. Her body shook and she opened her eyes, wide and dark, as he felt her wet release, and the shocking intimacy was the last assault on the teetering remnant of his control.

Pleasure rammed through him as he shattered along with her. He came with his eyes open, too, locked with her stunning gaze. One awesome burst of heat and he collapsed against her, slick where she was slick, still buried inside her.

Breaths slid by, and he would have moved off her but she kept her arms wrapped around him, clung as if he were some kind of salvation when he knew he was anything but. He just held her and breathed and wondered, oh God, what had he done? And he wanted to regret it, and tomorrow he would, but tonight he wasn't sane enough.

Finally, she let him go, and he slipped beside her, still working to steady his raging heart rate. She turned her cheek against his chest and he put his arm around her, held her tight and close and prayed to God he could keep her safer from the traitor in PAX than he'd kept her from himself.

For the first time in two years, Paige woke up exactly where she wanted to be—in a bed she'd shared with Kieran. Her eyes flashed open, a surge of vivid memory overtaking her. The bed beside her was empty, the room quiet, shadowed, morning sun peeking through a crack in the drapes.

That first honest thought, unmonitored by her saner self, hit her again. She wanted to wake up in a bed she'd shared with Kieran.

No. She clamped her hands over her face. No, that couldn't be how she felt. She'd gone to Callula Island for a divorce. She wanted a new life, a life without Kieran.

Her fingers slid down her face and she sat up, yanking the tangled sheet with her. There were her panties, across the floor. Her T-shirt lay in a heap nearby.

The shower came on, and she realized Kieran was in the bathroom. Thank God. She leaped up, grabbed the panties, stumbling into them then reaching for the

T-shirt. No way did she want Kieran to come out of his shower and find her naked. She tore the shirt over her head, down over her body.

She'd slept with him, but she didn't want him to see her naked. That made so much sense. *Good job keeping your head straight, Paige,* she berated herself.

She sat down on the end of the bed. Her knees were shaking. Dammit, what had she been thinking? Or *not* thinking, was more the question. Temporary insanity. That had to be the answer. She'd had the crazy idea that a goodbye kiss wasn't enough, that it was somehow unworthy of what they'd shared. So goodbye sex was the answer?

Make that *incredible* goodbye sex. But goodbye sex was still goodbye sex. It didn't change anything.

That was a lie, though. It changed everything. It made her remember all too clearly how much she missed his soft, tender kisses and the way they could turn into fiery passion in a heartbeat. She missed the way she could get beneath that hard, remote outer layer of his and make him beg.

Only she was the one who was going to end up begging. She was the one who didn't want things to end this way. Maybe she didn't want things to end in *any* way. *Don't leave me, Kieran. Don't ever leave me.*

How pathetic was that? But there was no denying it, no use continuing the lies. She'd slept with him, and the truth was so plain, even she couldn't pretend anymore. And now she was going to have to live with it. One episode of great sex did not a repaired marriage make.

The bathroom door opened and she nearly leaped out of her skin. She hadn't even realized the water had stopped running. And there he was, standing outside the bathroom with a towel wrapped around his waist, his hair wet, drops of water still trickling down his very broad chest.

She wanted to wake up with him every day, just like this. She wanted him to walk over and take her in his arms and do a repeat performance of last night. And what difference would it make? Things couldn't get worse. She couldn't wind up any more hurt, could she? She was already screwed.

A hiccup of half panic, half laughter, bubbled up in her throat at that too-literal thought.

He just stood there, staring at her with those dark, enigmatic eyes of his, as if he had something important to say. And like a sharp blade to her heart, realization hit her and she knew what was coming, and that yes, things could actually get worse. She bolstered the shreds of her courage. Her dignity was just about all she had left, and she still had a shot at salvaging that much.

"Don't worry," she fired off in the quiet tautness of the room. "If I'm pregnant, it's not your problem."

Chapter 10

She dropped that little bomb, then spurted off the bed, shoving past him toward the bathroom.

Kieran grabbed Paige's arm. She whipped around, but she wouldn't look at him. He was looking at her, though. Looking at her soft cheekline, the mold of her breasts against the thin cotton of her tee, the hint of panty peeking from between her thighs. The wave of yearning that hit him nearly had him ready to choke.

"What the hell is that supposed to mean?" he demanded, his voice coming out harsher than he intended. He lifted his gaze to her face.

Her heavy lashes lifted, slowly, and the eyes she'd hidden from him were controlled, distant.

"I mean, it's not your problem," she repeated matter-of-factly. "I'm fully aware that we didn't use protection last night, and if something comes of it, don't worry about it."

Frustration wrapped a sharp fist around his heart. "You're telling me to not worry about my *child?*"

"There is no child. And there probably won't be. We made a mistake. We were irresponsible. It's over and done, and there's no point crying over spilled milk now."

Spilled milk? What they'd had last night was spilled milk? Anger burned his throat, his eyes. But hadn't he been ready to come out here and tell her exactly the same thing? When what he really wanted to do was throw himself at her feet, tell her he'd missed her more than he'd known humanly possible, and that he'd never wanted last night to end?

But then, he wished for a lot of things that weren't possible. He had a single goal now, to find the person behind the lab explosion and destroy them. Detaching from Paige was part of that. But if there was a baby—

"A baby is a little bigger than spilled milk," he said, that damn fist clutching tighter on his heart. A baby, with Paige's eyes. A baby, who'd need him in a way he didn't want to be needed. A baby, who would probably never even know him because he'd probably be dead before it was born.

"I know you never wanted to have a baby with me," she said, and tried to jerk her arm away from him, "so I'd really rather we just forget it happened. If there is a baby, I'll handle it."

He did a double take and didn't let go. "Do you think I would want that? You think I wouldn't want to know my own child? You think I never wanted to have a baby with you?" He slammed the questions at her, and they slammed right back at him. He didn't want the answers.

Kieran wheeled away, but now she came after him.

"What else would I think? When I tried to talk about having a baby, you shut me out. You never even wanted to have the conversation."

He stood in front of the drapes, the sun slicing through stung his eyes. Or that's what he told himself. The ball growing in his chest told him something else.

"What kind of father do you think I would be, Paige?" His voice came out raspy. "I didn't have much of an example."

"How would I know? When did you ever tell me anything but the barest of bones about your father? When did you ever even let me meet him?"

The cool matter-of-fact tone was gone from her voice, and the aching tenderness just made him want her to go away. This wasn't a conversation they should be having. Maybe they should have had it before, but it was too late now.

Forcing himself, he turned and steeled himself against the concern and questions in her eyes. "Do you think I would have ever wanted you to meet him? He did just about everything a father can do to make a son's life hell. When I got out of prison, I never looked back. I don't know if he's alive or dead, and I don't want to know."

She took a step toward him, then another. Then she was touching him, her hand on his shoulder. "That's a lie. You do nothing but look back. You think you'd be a terrible father because of him. How does that make any sense?"

"It doesn't have to make sense, Paige. I can't risk it. I don't know what kind of father I'd make, but I know enough to know that you can't escape how you were brought up. When my five-year-old smarts off, I don't want to punch him so hard that he wakes up on the floor. I don't want him wondering if I ever loved him because I never told him. I don't want him taking the heat for a crime he didn't commit just to get the hell out my house."

Emotion balled higher. It was in his throat now and he couldn't trust himself to say anymore. He'd said too much already and the look on Paige's face was killing him.

Silence clung to the room for a long moment.

"You are not your father," she said fiercely. "You would make a great dad. You would never do any of those things to your child. I know it."

The pain in her eyes was for him, not herself, and that was so much worse. She actually believed he could be a great dad. She knew his past, and she knew what had happened to him that night in the lab, but she still wasn't accepting that he was changed forever. If there had been any hope for him, it was over.

"You don't know what I'm capable of now, Paige, and neither do I." He drew in a sharp breath, moved so that her hand fell away from his shoulder. "Like you said, it was a mistake. We were irresponsible. If we've made a baby, if I'm still alive when it's born, I'm not going to shirk my responsibilities. That's all I wanted you to know."

And how the hell he'd told her so much more, he didn't know. But sooner or later, she'd get it. Either he'd be dead, or he'd be trapped in the monster he'd become. And that monster didn't have a place in her minivan world she wanted to build.

She didn't move. She just kept standing there, staring at him as if she wanted to say something but couldn't get it out.

Then she spoke, and that was worse. "I lied."

He blinked. "What?"

"I lied. It wasn't a mistake. I wanted to make love to you."

His heart felt tight and sore.

"I wanted to find out—" She broke off, squeezed her eyes shut for an awful beat, then opened them and pure hurt blazed from them. "I wanted to find out if there was anything left between us besides all the anger and regret. And I think there is."

He shook his head, a desperate ache building in his heart. She'd started off nice and distant, and he'd blown it by letting loose with feelings he should have kept to himself. Now, her soft heart was filling with pity for him. No woman in her right mind would want him now, knowing what he was. Damn irony that he'd kept those feelings about his inability to be a father to himself for years, and now when his back was to the wall, somehow they'd spilled. But he couldn't let Paige's empathetic response make her think anything had changed.

"Your life is already in danger," he said. "And now I've put you in another kind of jeopardy. It *was* a mistake. More mine that yours. I don't want to restart our marriage, Paige. The bald fact is I used you last night. I took advantage of the comfort you offered, and I take full responsibility for whatever happens as a result, but it doesn't have anything to do with our marriage."

The tender look in her eyes hardened, and the satisfaction he wanted to take from that burned bile in his throat instead.

"Of course you take full responsibility," she said in a low, tense voice that didn't quite hide the thread of hurt. "You are single-handedly responsible for saving the world. I forgot for a minute."

She turned and walked to the bathroom, leaving him standing there feeling like the lowest creature on earth.

The hotel clerk told them where they could find a bus station. In the chill of the dawn, they walked inside and rented a locker where he stored the disk containing his research into the containment serum. The gun was in the pocket of his jacket, along with what remained of the still-damp cash.

A discount superstore on the highway heading out of town caught her attention. Clothes were an issue. Or maybe merely a distraction.

She could still feel Kieran's heat, his arms, his lips, his body pressed against hers. She tingled in secret places that only he had ever touched. Even her skin smelled of his musk.

He was in her system, down deep, at cellular level. Temporary insanity last night? She was crazy all the time when she was with him. She'd come damn close to pleading with him to give their marriage another chance this morning. That would have been stupid. How many times did he have to reject her before she got it?

"I need to get some things," she said quickly,

pointing at the store they were about to pass. "I can't keep wearing these same clothes. And these shoes are just trashed." Kieran's were, too. Ocean swimming hadn't done any of their attire any good.

Kieran made a quick turn and pulled into the sprawling parking lot of the superstore. Early shoppers straggled in through the banks of automatic doors from the near-empty parking lot.

"We can split up, if you want," she suggested once they got inside. "It'll be quicker." The men's and women's sections marched side by side on opposite aisles of the humongous store.

Kieran looked as if he might protest that suggestion for a second, but when she picked up a pair of skimpy cheetah-patterned panties off the rack behind her, his gaze grew hot and he walked away.

There was a small part of her that wanted to laugh at his discomfort, but an even larger part of her felt immensely sad. It sucked, this distance that time and hurt had forged between them. Since they'd left the hotel, they'd been pretending it hadn't happened, that it didn't matter. That it had been one big fat nothing.

It was a whopper of a lie. Her body hummed, her inside burned. What they'd shared had been stirring and shattering and nowhere close to nothing.

Taking a deep breath, she forced herself back into control. She was contained. She was cool. She was Ice Paige.

She shopped on automatic, grabbing several changes of T-shirts and jeans. A box of sturdy boots in her size rounded out her needs.

The shoe department was in the back of the store, stretching across a good third of the massive building. When she'd finished up, she looked up and down the shoe aisles for Kieran. Then she went to the men's clothing section.

He wasn't there, either.

Her pulse bumped up a notch. Her feet moved faster as she traced her path back to the shoe department. She rushed down every aisle, turning corners and rushing up the next one.

She came around a towering display of sandals and smashed into a hard, dangerous chest.

The scream she had to swallow made her feel like an idiot. Her knees were shaking ridiculously. So much for Ice Paige.

"Here you are," Kieran said, pulling back, his arms on her shoulders. "My God, are you okay?"

She knew her face was bloodless. It was crazy. She'd thought he was gone. She'd thought he'd taken off and left her. And that was pure foolishness. He was going to leave her at Buck's Run. Not in the middle of a discount superstore. She *knew* that.

But she was scared. Terrified. Deep down horror-movie-scream-in-her-throat frightened and it had nothing to do with what waited for Kieran back at PAX, nothing to do with him leaving her at Buck's Run.

She was falling in love with him. Again.

"I'm fine," she lied, stepping back. "I just didn't know where you were for a minute."

He gave her an odd look then took her purchases in his arms. After checking out at the front of the store, they stopped at the phone outside.

"Dub? Just checking in. Everything going okay?"

Paige waited, watching Kieran's lean, dangerous, in-control body leaning against the brick of the building. In control as she was not.

He hung up after a minute.

"He's fine," he said to her questioning eyes. "He should be at Buck's Run by tonight."

Everything was on track. Great. And she still didn't have a decent plan for stopping him.

He placed a call to Brian's cell, but there was no answer.

The parking lot was damp, puddled from the rain the day before. The pine-scented air felt heavy under the looming sky that threatened more storms.

They stopped for a fast-food breakfast then headed out, the early morning sun shedding pink-gold fairy rays on the dewy rural landscape along the quiet state highway. They were in the middle of nowhere, trees soaring around them broken by the occasional pasture and farmhouse.

She tried to not look at Kieran, but it didn't change anything. She could feel him beside her, sense his concern for her even in his taut focus on the vast uncertainty ahead.

A black SUV passed them traveling in the opposite direction. The Gremlin sped up. A speed limit sign flashed by.

"You're already going fifteen over," Paige said then she saw Kieran's face.

"That black SUV just whipped a U-turn," he said, glancing in the rearview mirror again.

Paige craned her neck to watch behind the Gremlin. The SUV was gaining on them at a dangerous pace. A movement at the passenger side window sent a bolt of adrenaline to her heart before Kieran even spoke.

"They've got weapons in the vehicle," he shouted. "Get down!"

Kieran hit the gas as hard as he could. He would have liked nothing better than to pull over and take out whoever was in that SUV with his bare fangs. But not with Paige by his side. And dammit, she wasn't getting down.

The road curved and the Gremlin careened around it. He scanned the landscape ahead, looking for an out. He couldn't stay ahead of them for long, not in the old pile of crap they were driving. They'd have to find some way to evade.

"Give me your gun," Paige demanded.

His insides knotted, but he was driving. He couldn't return fire if they had to. Paige had gone white as a sheet, but the grip that took the gun he handed over was steady.

She rolled her window down, ready. A shot shattered the rear window and Paige screamed. Then, damn her, she still wasn't getting down. She craned her arm out the window and returned fire.

The SUV was still gaining. There was no way they were going to beat it, not with the Gremlin's old engine. It was only the turns in the road that were keeping the men behind them from getting off another shot.

He gripped the steering wheel as he veered to take a sharp left down the side road. The SUV's tires screamed loudly as it stopped short, backed up, and peeled out after them.

The Gremlin popped in the air as it hit a pothole on the twisty one-lane road. A flock of geese scattered as they passed a broken-down trailer home in the woods. They flew over a low-water bridge. The road turned to gravel and rocks bounced back behind them.

Coming around another turn, a logging truck started pulling out of another side road.

Kieran gunned the engine.

His heart jumped into his throat as they barely cleared the massive truck. In the rearview mirror, he saw the logger stop for a beat, then the huge truck began to move again.

The SUV rounded the curve, swung to avoid the truck halfway into the road making its turn, and spun crazily. The Gremlin flew around another twist in the road and a sign pointing to a highway whipped by.

Paige had a death grip on the door handle of the Gremlin, the other hand still clutching the gun. A dirt road on the right looked like it went nowhere and that was just where he wanted to go. Mud from the recent rain flew up, splattering the side windows.

The Gremlin bumped and groaned over the narrow rutted road. Thick trees cloaked the sky then the road opened up to a vista of splintered tree stumps, a logging field. The car thumped to a stop at the end of the trail.

The engine died and there was no sound but his pounding heart. He looked at Paige. She was still holding on to the gun like it was molded to her fist.

He placed his hand over hers, felt the small coldness of it. But she was alive. That was all that mattered. And he had to keep her alive.

"I think we lost them," he said finally. He prayed to God he'd lost them. But he didn't doubt the SUV hadn't been stopped for long. As soon as they came out of the spin and got going again, they'd be looking for them. "They'll think we headed for the highway."

"We can't stay here all day," Paige pointed out.

Her blue eyes were huge and frightened, and now, finally, she was shaking, the aftermath setting in. She dropped the gun on the dash.

"We'll have to wait here for a little bit, long enough for them to head for the highway. Then we'll go back in the other direction, find another road to take." They were a long way from Buck's Run, and if they had to crisscross their way there, it was going to take a hell of a long time to arrive.

He pushed out of the small car, guessing what he'd find. They were safe, for now, but they had other problems to handle. The rear window was a spider's web of fractured glass with a neat round hole. But that wouldn't stop them from driving the car. There was another, bigger, problem.

Paige came out after him. The sound of cicadas filled the muggy air from the woods behind them. The view beyond of slashed trees contrasted in foreboding silence.

"Oh, my God. I hope there's a decent spare," she breathed.

The Gremlin's left rear tire was demolished. To top off their day, it started raining again. Wind shook the trees and drops danced down around them where they stood in the open.

"Get in the car," he said. "I'll fix it."

She gave him a look that needed no words to explain, but she didn't let that stop her.

"You know, I'm not a helpless daisy," she bit out. "I can help change a tire."

She could help him find the traitorous agent in PAX, too, was what she really wanted to say. He could see it in her stormy eyes. And what's more, he could see the way the drops dashing from above were soaking her T-shirt to her soft breasts. For a full minute, he just stood there, staring at the way her nipples poked hard and alert through the thin white material and all he could think about was how alive he'd felt in that hotel room when he'd held her in his arms.

Making love to her had been a mistake, and he still couldn't find the discipline to regret it no matter what he'd said to her about it. Even now he couldn't regret it. Because right now, he just wanted to make love to her all over again.

He belonged in an asylum, he was sure of it. They'd just been chased off the road by a mysterious SUV driven by people who'd like to capture him and kill Paige, and they were stuck who the hell knew where with a flat tire. And it was pouring.

And all he could think about was ripping Paige's damn wet T-shirt off and doing a whole lot more after that, like burying himself in her optimistic fantasy world where everything would work out. And he really didn't even need to be near her right now if he couldn't look at her without wanting to rip her clothes off.

"There's no point in both of us getting soaked," he pointed out. He turned away to look in the back of the Gremlin, to look anywhere but at her, but swerved back around at Paige's voice.

"Fine."

She stood there in the rain, glaring at him, her damn arms crossed over her tempting breasts now. She was soaked and spitting fire and he was confused as hell. She was saying fine but she didn't look like she meant it.

"Fix it yourself," she snapped at him darkly. "You can do everything by yourself, can't you? I'm sure you don't need me."

"Goddammit, Paige." He strode toward her, but stopped short at the flicker of pain in her eyes that he didn't know what to do with.

"Just fix the damn tire," she said, her voice calm and controlled now despite the rigid anger in her stiff shoulders.

The tangible heat of her fury staggered him. He knew she didn't like his plans, knew she hated that he wouldn't include her, wouldn't put her in danger. And she had a hell of a lot more to be angry about, too. She had two years' worth of pain built up.

And right now, she looked like a volcano about to erupt.

"Go ahead, fix the tire, Kieran," she repeated in a low, tense voice he wouldn't have been able to make out over the increasing rain if not for his super sensitive hearing.

He stared at her, a little overwhelmed, a lot frustrated, and went back to the business at hand, his own anger boiling to the surface. In furious jerks, he pulled out the pitiful undersize spare in the back of the Gremlin, and just about fell over in relief when he found a beat-up jack.

It wasn't till he put the ruined tire in the back and threw in the jack, wet as if he'd taken a dive in the ocean again, that he looked up and realized Paige was completely gone.

Chapter 11

He'd almost had a heart attack by the time he found her sitting in what had slowed to a steady drizzle by a creek a few yards through the thick hardwoods. She was huddled on a fallen log, staring down at the plops splashing into the meandering stream.

"Don't disappear on me like that," he ground out.

She jerked her head around. Her eyes stabbed him. "Oh, really? It bothers you when I disappear?"

Hot irritation threaded his veins. "You should have gotten in the car."

"Why? Am I going to get wetter?" She turned back around, just sat there, arms crossed around herself, shoulders stiff. "I'm already soaked. I've sat in that car enough for the past twenty-four hours. Tell me when you're done fixing the tire all by your big, bad super-agent self and I'll get back in."

Her mood had apparently not improved in the twenty minutes he'd been working on the tire. Well, his mood hadn't improved, either. He was soaked and getting more soaked by the second.

He started down the mossy, fern-covered slope to the creek, ready to shake some sense into her.

"I'm done fixing the tire, Paige, and you know it. And you're not upset because I suggested fixing the tire myself."

Now she turned around. "You're right." She got off the log and straightened. "For once." She marched up the slope toward him, meeting him halfway. "I'm angry because you are so busy trying to save me that you haven't given one second's thought to saving yourself."

They stood there, both of them blazing heat despite the damp chill. Her hair was smashed to her head, little golden strands of it caught damply on her smooth cheeks. Rain dripped down her face. That T-shirt from hell was stuck to her chest like it was a second skin.

"I don't want you to be hurt," he said helplessly.

"I'm already hurt," she yelled at him. "And I'm going to hurt even more if you don't make it out of this alive. Maybe you'd see that if you weren't so caught up in trying to save the world on your own."

Why did she keep saying that? Was that what she thought he was doing? Trying to save the world? As if he could.

"You don't have to take care of me," she charged on. "When are you going to get that through your thick head? You aren't going to be responsible if anything happens to me. *I'm* the only who is responsible for me."

The emotion-charged air hung staticky between them. Rain tap-tapped on the trees. He could almost hear the pulse thundering in Paige's angry blood.

"You're in this danger because of me. Dammit, Paige, we're soaking wet. Let's get the hell out of—"

She marched up the bank, pushed back him, then pivoted back. "Why did you marry me?"

His mind went blank for an answer to something that was so out of the blue, he couldn't think straight.

"Because you asked me," he said, and that was a lie but it fell off his lips too quickly.

Heat and pain flared in her eyes, and there was no taking them back. There was no time.

"Go to hell," she hissed, and she reached out with her hand. He thrust out his arm to stop her, held tight to her trembling fingers. When he was sure she wouldn't hit him, he let go.

"I didn't mean that," he said, anguish banding his

chest at the dark hurt in her lovely eyes. She looked abused, and he was the abuser.

Misery stabbed him.

"Yes," she said in a low, thick voice. "You did." With that, she pushed past him.

Kieran's heart turned over and he went after her. "Paige—"

She ran, and he made chase, grabbing at her arm and whipping her around as she reached the car. She stumbled, but he held her upright, kept her from falling. She was out of breath, her eyes wild and dark. Her chest heaved, and rain and tears mingled together on her cheeks. Paige retreated, her back bumping up against the side of the car. He wouldn't let go of her, afraid she'd run again.

"Stop running. I didn't mean that the way it came out." God, he had to make her believe him and he didn't know if he could. "I married you because I loved you, Paige. Even when I didn't want to, even when I thought it wasn't fair to you."

"Fair to me?" Her eyes flared shock and hurt burned raw in her voice. "Since when does love have to be fair?"

He didn't know how to answer her question. Or maybe he didn't want to know.

"Love is not fair," she said fiercely. "You can't control who you love. It's just there, like the sun coming out in the morning. You can't stop it. God knows I tried enough times. I tried every time I fell in love with a new foster family and they didn't love me back. Not enough to give me a permanent home." She stopped, chewed her lip, her liquid eyes turning away from him for a beat.

He couldn't stop himself. He reached up, touched her chin, drew her gaze back to him. There were tears in her eyes, and he felt the answering emotion in his throat.

"I did love you, Paige." Past tense. He saw the flinch in her eyes. She noticed, too. And words rose in his clogged throat, words he couldn't get out.

"Then why did you always push me away?" she asked softly. "Why did you have to be running for your life before you could tell me the truth about how you felt about having kids? Why do you tell me I'm a great PAX agent with one breath and refuse to let me help you with the next? Why did you marry me as a PAX agent then fight me every inch of the way over the risks I took in my research?"

Every one of her questions stung a knife into him. Everything she said was true about how he'd treated her during their marriage. He'd pushed her away at every turn.

"I don't know what makes me do that," he said roughly. "I know that I do it. I know I pushed you away, and I couldn't stop. It's the way I am, and that's not a good enough answer, I know that. When

I was in college, I dated a girl named Danica. She was the only other real relationship I had before I met you. We dated for about a year. She wanted to get serious, and I started accusing her of seeing other guys."

"Was she?"

He shook his head. "I wasn't even jealous. I *knew* she wasn't seeing anyone else. There was nothing to be jealous *of*."

"She broke it off?" Paige guessed, watching him.

He nodded. "I pushed her away."

There was another long beat. Wind rustled in the trees. He tore his gaze from Paige, worked to control the stew of feelings inside him. Feelings too close to the surface.

"You wanted to see if she would go," Paige said suddenly.

He snapped his gaze back to her.

"You pushed her away to see if she'd go," Paige repeated. "You pushed me away to see if I'd go." Tears glistened in her eyes. "That's what you do. You push people away, before they can hurt you. Before they can not love you like your father, or die on you like your sister. But I'm not going to go away, Kieran. You can push all you want, but I'm not going."

God, that couldn't be true. That was like some kind of test. If that was true, he was just sick and cruel.

"That's crazy," he said, his chest tight. Her eyes were so intensely blue, so glued on him with painful belief. She was reading way too much into what he'd said. "If you think that's what's going on now, you're wrong. You're dreaming."

"And you're lying," she flung at him, and tears coursed down her cheeks now, but she ignored them. "We don't know how much time we have left. Can't you be honest with me for once? Stop pushing me away. Don't take me to Buck's Run. Take me with you."

"I *am* being honest with you!" He felt as if he could barely breathe. All the hot emotion he felt for Paige was filling up his throat. He had to bury it, where it was safe, where it couldn't hurt Paige. "Can't you see that I'm trying to do the right thing here? I'm doing this for you."

"Doing what for me? Getting yourself killed?"

"No!" he exploded. "Keeping you safe."

"I'm not Annelie," she said fiercely. "It won't be your fault if anything happens to me. It wasn't your fault that anything happened to her."

He reached around her, tried to grab the handle of the car door.

She wouldn't move out of the way.

"Who's running now?" she demanded.

"I'm not running," he growled. "But we need to get on the road."

"Why do you blame yourself for Annelie's death?" she persisted. "Why does it have to be all on *your* shoulders?"

There was a long, long moment before he answered.

"Because," he said finally, "I was the one holding her. And I let go. That one's pretty damn simple."

"Could you have held on any longer?"

"She shouldn't have died," he said without answering her question. "And she wouldn't have if I hadn't let go."

He stopped, and the horrible image that day in that raging river poured over him. His arms had been burning. Annelie had been screaming. But he wouldn't allow himself any excuses, not even his underdeveloped twelve-year-old muscles.

"She was swept away in a river. Your father was high. He drove onto a washed-out bridge. That's why Annelie died. But you've turned it into something else in your head. Something else that lets you push people away."

Kieran felt a piercing warning shouting through his blood. She wasn't going to let that theory of hers go. But even if all of that was true, it didn't change the fact that he had to push her away now. He wouldn't be responsible for the death of someone he loved again. This time, if it had to be anyone, it would be him.

Her determined eyes held him. The tears that had fallen dried in tracks on her cheeks. "When this is over—"

"It's not going to be over, so none of this matters. My career is ruined. Maybe I can prove my innocence, but I'll never escape the cloud of suspicion. People will always wonder how much I knew, why that lab exploded, what I was really doing on that island. I don't have anything to lose here, but you do."

"There's your life," she whispered, raw. "You could lose your life if you don't stop pushing me away."

She said that like his life mattered, and the feelings roiling inside him like an avalanche about to overcome his common sense. Pushing her away was the last thing he wanted to do. He kissed her with all the searing need inside him. He tasted her tears and grief, and he wished he could change everything.

His hands tangled in her hair, skimming down the perfect curve of her sides. Her lips were needy, coaxing, her hips rocking into his, offering love, offering acceptance. Unconditional. Nowhere near fair.

"God, Paige," he rasped when he could, and he had no idea if he was praying for divine intervention or begging her not to stop.

He felt as if he was going to die from all the emotions inside him, and he could hardly breathe, much less think, when her hands slipped beneath his wet shirt, curving around his back.

She rocked against him again, a slight movement only, and yet it threatened to melt his bones away. He had one arm banding her hip, the other supporting the back of her head as he kissed her again, and again. When he finally tore away, her dark gaze met his, soft with heat and arousal. He felt like he was coming off some kind of drug, and he wanted more of it.

Her nipples were hard, pebbling against the wet material of her shirt, and he needed so desperately to touch them the way he'd touched them last night. Raindrops slid down her cheeks and she'd never looked so beautiful to him. The air was thick and sweet with pine and the bitter scent of hope just beyond his reach.

"I want to make love to you again," she said, and her eyes were wide open and honest. There was a trace of fear there, too.

He wanted to take that fear away, so badly. But he couldn't give her what she needed. He never could. "We can't make that mistake again." He skimmed her cheek with his hand and stood back. "I want you to have that minivan and you'll never have it with me."

Mountains scraped the sky, with crystal clear stream valleys cutting the earth, but as the dusk fell over the Shenandoah River, Paige had nothing inside her to appreciate the picturesque views. They were closing in on Buck's Run, and Kieran thought that just like that, it would be over. He was going to hand her over to another man's care like she was a parcel to be delivered. Her blood simmered with frustration and grief. She didn't have a plan, but no way was she staying there. If she could, she'd convince Dub to help her change Kieran's mind. If she couldn't, she'd go after him on her own. Somehow.

She wasn't going to be pushed away, and she just had to pray to God that she was right about what he was doing and that she wasn't making a bigger fool out of herself than ever.

They'd driven for hours with few stops, staying off the state highways now, sticking to two-lane rural roads. They'd picked up some supplies for the cabin, and he'd checked in with Dub. He was already at Buck's Run by the time they called, and all was clear.

He'd called his friend, Scott, too, but Scott hadn't had any information for him yet. Hacking into every bank in D.C. to find the records Kieran needed was going to take more time. He'd called Brian, too, to check in about their meeting. Brian hadn't picked up.

They turned down a dirt road, narrow and overhung with trees. The rain had stopped but the darkening woods were gloomy and damp around them. The A-frame cabin appeared at a turn in the lane. Dub's worn-out pickup sat in front of the cabin.

Kieran pulled the Gremlin onto the grass and parked it around back. The light on the back door was lit. As he turned off the engine, Dub opened the door and waved.

The cabin was minimally but comfortably furnished. There were two bedrooms, one a loft and the other downstairs. The kitchen was stocked with pots and pans, and Dub, with his bulging, tattooed muscles, greased-back ponytail and black T-shirt and jeans, looked more like a biker than a commercial fisherman. Or whatever else he was in his spare time. He was a little mysterious, a little dangerous, and thoroughly competent-looking.

Despite his utterly non-domestic appearance, he fried burgers and watched Paige with curious eyes as they worked together to prepare a quick dinner.

"It's good to see the two of you together," he commented to Kieran while Paige poured out glasses of Coke in the plastic cups they'd bought at the store on the way in.

"I'm leaving in the morning," Kieran said.

Dub put the last burger on a plate. "When will you be back?"

"I won't be."

Paige's stomach tightened.

"Can I help?" Dub asked.

"Yes," Paige interjected. "Kieran seems to think he needs to save the world by himself, and I disagree so I won't be staying. You can help by convincing him that he needs me."

Kieran cast her a dark look, then turned back to Dub. "You've helped enough. And so has she. I'm counting on you to make sure you both stay alive—and at Buck's Run."

They sat down at the table, and Dub leaned back

in the ladder-back chair. He looked like he really didn't want to get in the middle of their argument. "I figure you wouldn't be here if you weren't in a hell of a lot of trouble." He glanced at Paige. "I hope I didn't cause that trouble by telling Paige where you were."

"It isn't your fault. I owe you everything," Kieran said. He hadn't taken a bite yet. He looked pale beneath his island-dark skin. His eyes were fatigued, and worry curled into the frustration banding Paige's chest. "I don't want anything to happen to you, or to Paige. You're both accomplices already simply by being with me."

Dub lifted one big shoulder in a shrug. "You didn't do anything wrong."

A shadow of emotion crossed Kieran's rigid expression. "You don't know that."

"I know you." For Dub, it was that simple.

For Kieran, nothing was simple. He accepted Dub's loyalty because he had no choice, but she knew he hated the danger Dub was in because of him, just as he hated the danger she was in. She thought about that kiss back in the woods before they'd headed for Buck's Run again. It had been so full of risky emotion that Kieran wouldn't acknowledge. He loved her, he *had* to love her. How else could he have kissed her that way?

No matter what he believed, she knew that what tied them together was unbreakable. But he wouldn't admit it, nor would he admit that he had any chance at all for a future, much less one with her. He was too busy pushing her away.

Rejection wasn't new to her. Inside, she was always that ten-year-old girl who feared that the only people who would ever truly love her were dead. And no matter how she fought and how she hoped, at the last she always backed down. Always protected herself. She'd done it with Kieran, time and again, and it had taken seeing him again to make her face it. She'd let him push her away in the past.

And if she sat here in this cabin and let him push her away, she'd be doing the same thing all over again. She'd thought loving him was the risk she shouldn't repeat. She'd been wrong. She hadn't loved him *enough.*

"This conversation is a waste of time." Paige pushed back, got out of her chair. "I'm going to change my clothes, and when I come out—" she gave Kieran a hard look "—if you're gone, I'm going to follow you."

His jaw tightened. She turned her back on him and grabbed the bags of her things she'd brought in.

No sooner had she straightened than something shattered. She whirled in shock, saw the broken front window of the cabin, something small and cylindrical tumble across the pine-planked floor.

A bomb. Her stunned mind froze for a split second.

"Get down," she screamed, but Kieran was already there, already on top of her, rolling with her away from the bomb.

The explosion ripped through the cabin, deafening. Fire licked around them. Dub was running, and in his hand was a gun. Kieran dragged Paige into his arms, dashing for the door, escape.

But escape to what?

Outside, the night sky was alive with flame and gunfire. Dub raced for his truck, shooting with both barrels.

God, he had *two* guns.

They were in the trees. Whoever had thrown that bomb was in the trees, waiting for them.

"Get out of here, Dub! Go, Paige!" Kieran shouted, shooting with one hand and pushing her through the smoky air and fire toward Dub's truck with the other.

But she clutched at him, wouldn't let go. Terror-locked gazes held. A shot arrowed past her ear. And he had no choice. She wasn't giving him one. He wasn't going to go with Dub and put his cousin in more danger, and she wasn't going to go with Dub, either.

Paige felt every beat of her heart as she tore with Kieran toward the Gremlin. The cabin spit fire and the sound of Dub's engine roared through the air. He was still shooting, covering them, she realized.

They raced for the Gremlin and tore open the

doors. Then they were inside, the cantankerous old car leaping to life, and they tore out down the dirt road, Dub's truck giving chase.

She was shaking. She'd never shaken so hard in her life, and her heart was lodged so thickly in her throat, there was no way she could speak. Her lungs burned as the small car bumped and flew over the ruts and potholes in the road.

He changed roads, heading down a different gravel lane that she realized was a shortcut to the highway. They'd lost Dub by the time they got to the main road. No one else was behind them.

Yet.

"What about Dub?" she breathed hoarsely.

"He's better off nowhere near me," Kieran rasped. "And so are you. Dammit, Paige."

They passed a series of businesses. Light flashed into the car, and it was then she saw the crimson streak down his arm.

She gasped. "You've been shot."

"Are you all right? Are you cut anywhere? Burned?" His gaze scraped her, worried for her.

"I'm fine," she said impatiently. "Pull over. We have to take care of your shoulder."

"I'm all right," he said. "But we need to ditch the Gremlin. I don't know if they followed us to the cabin, or Dub, but I've had it with this car."

He drove into a truck stop, pulling around to the back. The place was lively despite the late hour.

"They're going to be looking for us. I don't know how much time we have." He started to reach for his things in the back of the car then winced.

Paige reached back and got the bag from the discount superstore.

"We have to go in," she said. "We have to get some towels. You need a doctor!"

"No. No doctors. It's just a flesh wound, I'm sure of it." But he looked pale and awful just the same. "I'll call Dub on his cell and make sure he's all right."

Irritation broke through the aftermath of panic. Paige got out of the car and went inside to the restroom, tearing off several paper towels and wetting them. There was a restaurant inside along with a small convenience store inside where she was able to pick up some bandages. When she came back, Kieran was putting the phone back down in the booth.

"Dub's all right," he said. "Thank God."

The weary pain in his eyes stabbed her heart and she didn't have it in her to yell at him about refusing to see a doctor. They went back to the car and carefully, she peeled off Kieran's shirt, lifting it over his head then down off the injured shoulder.

She went to work using the damp towels she'd gotten from the restroom.

"See?" he said when she cleaned away the blood. "Flesh wound."

He was right, but it was a nasty one. They were both incredibly lucky that they'd gotten out without being burned. And even luckier that Dub had shot their way out to their cars, holding their cover long enough for them to drive away from whoever had been waiting in the woods.

Her fingers were still trembling as she placed the bandage over the cleaned wound.

"We have to get out of here," Kieran said. "We're too close to the cabin. They'll be looking for us here."

He managed to get a new shirt on, the strained lines of his face revealing the discomfort it caused him to move his shoulder. The bandage was hidden beneath the fresh black tee. And still, beyond the pain and exhaustion, he was nothing but hard chiseled strength, damp and smelling like smoke and pine and deadly intent.

"Paige—"

She waved a frustrated hand at him, her temper rising at the words she knew he was about to say.

"Don't tell me you've got someplace else you're going to leave me," she cut him off. "Don't ask me to walk away. Someone has tried to kill me four times in the past two days, and someone's after you who's not going to stop. I'm seeing this through to the end whether you like it or not."

Chapter 12

Kieran saw a determination in Paige's eyes that scared him. He hated the danger she was in, hated that it was his fault. He wanted to protect her and she wouldn't let him.

She wouldn't walk away.

"God, Paige," he groaned as he reached out to touch her sweet face. "That's just it. You could have been killed so many times already."

"But I wasn't killed. I'm okay, and so are you."

She leaned in and kissed him, softly, on his mouth, making him feel alive. All he'd thought about for two years was his death. Paige had the power to make him dream of life. She was getting inside him, waking up hopes and dreams that should have been lost.

"And we're going to stay okay," she whispered against his lips, and as she pulled away, he saw determination and will in her eyes. "Together. There is no safe place for me, and you know that. So take me with you. Or leave me behind and watch me follow."

She'd do that. That hadn't been an empty threat back in the cabin. She'd follow him. And that should have made him want to scream in rage, but he couldn't get anything past the swell of an emotion that was the complete opposite of anger.

The aching silence filled the car.

"You can't push me away, Kieran," she said quietly now. "You're willing to die for me. I feel the same about you. Get over it."

And he saw again the flicker of vulnerability within that determination. The fear that he would reject her, ditch her, leave her behind even here in this damn truck stop. And he felt his own sick regret that she would even think he would do anything like that. She'd shown him over and over since she'd arrived on Callula Island that she trusted him. No one in their right mind *should* trust him, but Paige did.

He couldn't push her away, no matter what he or anyone else did or said. And he *was* a sick son of a bitch because she was right. That's what he'd been doing. Pushing her away to see if she'd go. And what it meant that in all these years, she'd been the only one to see through that lie that he'd lived even to himself, he couldn't handle thinking about right now.

"Get your things," he said with emotion so raw in his throat he could barely speak over it. "We're leaving the Gremlin here."

He went back to the pay phone and called Scott. Paige watched him, waited, and his gut tightened as Scott gave him the information. If this information meant what he thought it meant, he knew who the traitor was, and he was going to need a lot more proof than he'd realized.

"What did he have for you?" Paige asked.

God, he hated to tell her.

"Large deposits over a two-year period from an overseas bank," he said. "Someone's been promising something to a foreign agency, and they're getting paid for it." And he was betting it was the serums. His throat felt thick and he put his hand on Paige's shoulder. "It's Talia."

She paled. "No."

"We need more proof."

Vinn wasn't going to want to believe his own daughter was a traitor. Paige didn't want to believe it, either. The hurting shimmer in her eyes told him how much she didn't want this to be true.

He tried Brian's number again.

"Brian?"

An eerie finger crawled up his neck at the long silence.

"No, this isn't Brian." The voice was a husky whisper.

"Where's Brian?" he asked. "What are you doing with his phone?"

Paige leaned in close.

"Brian's dead."

Kieran's heart thumped at the look on Paige's face. She stood back.

"That's Talia's voice," she whispered starkly. "What's she doing with Brian's phone?"

"Kieran?" came the shocked whisper from the phone.

She'd recognized his voice, too.

Through the windows into the diner and then out onto the front lot, they could see a black SUV pull off the road, moving slowly, then the SUV headed for the back of the building.

It hadn't taken long. They were cruising the highway, looking for the Gremlin.

Dread pumped Kieran's blood. He slammed down the phone and grabbed Paige's hand. They raced inside the restaurant. An eighteen-wheeler with the logo Armstrong Independent Trucking sat in the lofty overhang of the truck refueling center in the front of the building. In tiny letters beneath the logo it read *Silver Spring, Maryland.* The door of the elongated cab hung open. Beyond, nothing but dark, soaring mountains. And behind them, on the other side of the building, lay trouble.

The truck driver wasn't in sight, but the clink of the fueling tank turning off shot the air. He'd intended to hitch a ride. He'd intended to ask first.

Paige's frantic eyes met Kieran's, the decision spilt-second. He pushed her ahead of him as they sprinted into the cab, over the driver's seat and up into the curtained-off sleeping compartment. Pain from his wounded shoulder sliced into his vision, almost blinding him. They could hear something slam at the back of the truck as the driver prepared to head out.

They whisked the drape shut behind them. He could feel Paige's heart pounding in the near-dark of the cramped compartment. She was pressed against the rear of the bunk, with Kieran's body against her. He rocked into her, easing his position, his arm banding over her to steady himself on the narrow bed.

A grunt of someone hiking up into the driver's seat cracked the silence then the tractor-trailer roared to life. Country-western music blared from the cab's sound system.

Kieran could only take so much. The pain of his shoulder didn't mask the experience of Paige's breasts pressing up to him, and the rumble of the truck's engines making her body feel as if it were quivering against him. He could feel her heart still thumping, and he stroked his hand down her back, meaning to soothe her as well as hang on, but he had to stop the stroking action or he'd lose it. He'd lose it in a deep, wet, messy kiss and then things would just get worse from there. Emotions were still too raw inside him to be trusted, and it would be too easy now to bury them in something that would make him forget.

He tried to reach for the cash in his jacket pocket, but he knew he couldn't get it out and still hang on. He was good and plastered against Paige, one arm stuck painfully beneath him and the other hanging on for dear life to keep from falling right out of the compartment onto their trucker friend's head. He slid his arm back around Paige for support.

"Get the cash," he breathed into her ear.

She shifted, which just caused him to overheat that much more, and lifted her head to meet his eyes in the dim, her mouth an inch away from his. Her brows drew together, then she made a barely perceptible nod and slid her hand between them again, grazing across his chest. He held on while she dug in his pocket, past the gun, and pulled out some money.

"I'm going to climb over you so you can get out," he told her. "Show him the cash."

Her eyes widened. "Why me?"

"You're cuter."

She made a soft snort, but worked with him as he

managed to shift over her and roll her to the other side of the compartment so that they'd switched positions. For a long beat, she hesitated. He knew she couldn't be eager for this little confrontation. The trucker was in for a surprise, and they just had to pray he'd take it well. But Paige was a rock, even when she was nervous. And she *was* cuter. She had a better shot at gaining the guy's trust and fast than Kieran did.

He heard her take an even breath, blow it out then she pushed out of the compartment in one quick move, landing partly on the console between the truck's two roomy seats. The trucker swung his head toward her and the tractor-trailer swerved at the shocked reaction from his hands on the wheel.

Paige shoved the cash at him. "Please help me."

"What the hell—" The man steadied the rig while reaching between the seats.

A jolt of panic raced to Kieran's heart. He reached for the gun in his jacket pocket, ready to do whatever he had to do.

The trucker stuck a gun in Paige's face. "Who the hell are you and how did you get in my rig?"

Paige dropped the cash on the console and scrunched back into the corner of the passenger seat as far away as possible from the gun.

"I don't want any trouble," she said quickly, speaking over the blaring music. "I have money. Take it. I just want a ride. That's all. We were at the truck stop and—"

"We?" the trucker exploded, rearing his head around to look into the back. Kieran kept his hand on the gun inside his pocket.

"He's my husband," Paige rushed on. "Please don't hurt us. My ex-boyfriend, he's not over me. Jack and I got married last month and my ex threatened to kill him. He followed us and he blocked our car in at the truck stop. We were so scared. Please help us."

She looked at Kieran. "Jack, tell him."

The trucker was still holding the gun on Paige. He hit the stereo button and cut off the croon of LeAnn Rimes. The sound of the engine humming filled the cab.

"I don't want that son of a bitch to hurt Annie," Kieran said, keeping his eyes steady on the trucker, who kept glancing back and forth from the dark road.

The man looked to be in his mid-forties, and the hand holding the gun was shaking badly. A vein popped in his forehead.

"We've got money," Kieran went on. "We can pay. We just need a ride." The truck was at least heading in the right direction. He'd on-ramped to the interstate and they passed a sign that read, Washington, D.C., 75 miles. "We had all our stuff shipped to D.C. a few days ago," he improvised, "and we're moving there. If we can get out of here, maybe we'll be okay. Maybe he'll forget about Annie."

"Please," Paige added softly. "We won't be any trouble. I'm sorry about stowing away. We didn't have time to ask. He drove up to the truck stop. God knows what he was going to do. He's crazy. He might have shot innocent people in the restaurant. He has a gun. We've tried the police. We've filled out a dozen reports against him. We can't get a restraining order. His daddy is a judge—"

"Holy shit," the trucker breathed. "Are you people for real?"

"I swear, we're for real. We're in trouble. If we don't get away, something terrible is going to happen. Please!" Paige managed to look like she was about to cry.

Then Kieran realized her emotion *was* real. She was looking straight at him now, and that pain of hers was so palpable, he knew she wasn't faking it. His chest felt tight.

The trucker swore again. He put the gun between his jean-clad thighs and picked up the cash, counting it while he held onto the wheel.

The man looked back at Paige and then at Kieran. "All right," he said, his voice wary as he stuffed the cash in shirt pocket. "But I've got a schedule, you know? I'm off-loading in Arlington then I'm heading home. I don't have time to take you anywhere special."

"That's okay." Paige gave the guy a wobbly smile. "Close enough."

"Thank you," Kieran put in.

"I want you up here," the trucker ordered Kieran. "Where I can see you. She can go back there."

The trucker picked up the gun again while Kieran shifted into the passenger seat. Paige scooted around and his arms banded her. Her waist was slender, her hips willowy. A perfect combination of softness and muscle. Softness and muscle that was rocking against him with every purring hum of the big rig's engine. He didn't want to let her go, but he did.

Paige settled into the rear compartment again.

"What about your car?" the trucker asked. "Aren't you going to have to go back and get that?"

"It was a junker." That, Kieran thought, was at least one truth in their pack of lies. "No big loss." The only way they were going to lose these gunmen after them was to ditch the Gremlin.

The trucker turned the radio back on, setting the volume lower.

"God, you people scared the hell out of me," he said after a minute. "I'm Frank, by the way."

Kieran looked him straight in the eye. "You're our new hero, Frank."

Despite the fact that Frank had said he wouldn't go out of his way for them, by the time they reached the D.C. area, he agreed to drop them off near a Metrorail station where they took the airport stop. Paige pulled out of the long-term parking lot in her practical Saturn, a sense of surrealism hitting her as she negotiated the familiar, heavily trafficked roads into the city. It was past 11:00 p.m.

Bright streetlights whipped by, flashing light and shadow into the small sedan. She'd left Washington days before, never expecting to return like this, exhausted and scared, with Kieran by her side.

A glance Kieran's way revealed the relentless fatigue carved in his hard features. They'd been shot at, crashed a helicopter, evaded a car chase and escaped a bombing, and there was no telling what else awaited them now. There was no emotion on his face, just a grim resolution that terrified her.

They hit the 14th Street bridge.

"Do you want to stop, get something to eat?" she asked. Not that she was hungry. She didn't even think she could swallow food at this point, her stomach was in such knots. But they were driving toward PAX and so much that was unknown.

She really didn't want to get where they were going. She wanted to turn around, go in the opposite direction.

"No," Kieran answered her, his low voice unyielding. "There's no stopping now."

They reached the heart of official Washington.

Museums, memorials, government headquarters slid by as she negotiated the still-busy avenue. Kieran removed the gun from his jacket pocket. Paige's pulse kicked up a notch in reaction.

Kieran climbed into the backseat. The Saturn's rear area was compact and she knew he would be cramped for the final minutes of their drive.

Her mouth felt dry, her throat tight as she turned into the entrance and stopped at the security station. A familiar, young guard leaned out the window. He was one of her favorites, Tom Wiley.

She prayed he didn't glance behind her seat where Kieran quietly crouched. She deliberately didn't pull up as far as usual to give him less of a view.

"Good evening, Miss Holt," he greeted her. "Working late and on the weekend to boot."

Paige forced a shrug and a tired smile.

"How's that baby doing, Tom?" They'd taken up a collection around the office for shower gifts for Tom's wife and new daughter a few weeks before. "Got any new pictures?"

"Of course." Tom tapped the guard post window. A fuzzy-headed cherub of an infant beamed out of the photo taped there.

"She's adorable." Paige smiled again. Tom clicked the button that lifted the gate. "Thanks, Tom."

She eased the Saturn down the ramp into the garage, turning around the first curve, easing down again onto another level. The garage was nearly empty at this time of night. She found a spot near the elevator and parked, killing the ignition.

Nothing stirred in the quiet of the well-lit garage. Paige's heart beat loud in her ears.

"All right," she said softly.

Kieran sat up and pushed open the car door. He gripped the gun tightly against his body, reaching for Paige quickly as she slid out.

He walked close to her, his powerful arm banding her waist. She punched the button for the elevator. The doors opened immediately, closing behind them as they stepped inside.

In the low light of the elevator, Paige leaned into the innocuous-seeming, unmarked panel that held the bio-read technology. Placing one eye level with the pinprick-size camera installed in the panel, she gave it the second it took to digitally calculate the position, orientation, and spatial frequency of her iris while the face-scan matched her biometric characteristics against PAX's top-secret database. She placed her palm against the fingerprint sensor.

Rather than heading up to the ten marked floors that made up the PAX League's offices that were open to the public, the elevator glided soundlessly, automatically, downward.

Words tangled in her heart. In seconds, the doors would open onto the main floor of the secret layer of the PAX League—the offices, laboratories, conference rooms, and covert headquarters dedicated to leading the world into a new era of defense against global terror.

But tonight, the terror was here, in the dark quiet of the PAX League building, just beyond those soundless elevator doors.

They would also be watched every second on surveillance cameras. If the security officer watching the display noticed that two people had approached the elevator, one person had accessed the bio-read, and now two people were entering the floor, it might not take any triggers in the system at all for them to investigate.

Tailgating between agents was technically against the rules, but it happened and wasn't an automatic cause for alarm during the course of a busy workday. But it was nearly 10:00 p.m. on a weekend. Hardly bustling business hours. On their side was the fact that the security station held multiple cameras—and they might, just might, make it past the main security station before the officer connected the dots.

She could hear nothing in the eerie silence of the parking garage except the thump-thump of her pulse pounding in her ears. Kieran's grip on her arm tightened and the hot ball of dread in her throat rose as the elevator doors slid open.

Chapter 13

The subterranean level of PAX stretched ahead of them, corridors with meeting rooms, offices, and laboratories striking off in several directions. A security station lay central to the compact lobby, the bank of surveillance equipment lining the walls of the glassed-in office.

Kieran stood just outside the range of the security officer's vision inside the elevator. Paige leaned snug against him, pretended to search through her jacket pockets as she used her foot to hold open the elevator door.

She waited for the officer to visually ID her and

then return to viewing the various monitors. The officer looked up and she waved then rustled through her pockets again, keeping a furtive eye on the station.

A long beat passed. "Now," she whispered.

Kieran pushed her out ahead of him, spying the officer, back turned as he made a notation on his log book of the agent entering the floor. In the low light of the nighttime lobby, Kieran and Paige raced beyond the station's immediate view.

His old office was on a wing off the main block. He'd shared it with Phil, and just walking down that hall hit Kieran with memories he couldn't handle right now.

He shut down the part of his brain that dealt in emotion. He couldn't afford to think in terms of friendship and betrayal, pain and loss.

But harder to dismiss were the cell-ripping, shattering and broken visions from that night. He'd torn in shock and horror from the lab, his skin bursting with agony. Alarms had pierced the floor. He remembered, as if from a nightmare, people tearing past him toward the lab.

In the bedlam, he'd kept running and running and running…

Somehow he'd made it out of the building. And then the next thing he'd known, it was dawn in the park and his life had forever changed.

Anger and a sick dread filled his throat as they approached the office door. The corridor expanded in both directions, silent and low-lit, bisecting another short hallway at the end where his office door was located. Around the corner, that short hallway led to his sealed lab.

Just as he prayed they wouldn't run head-on into another agent pulling a late night on the weekend, from back up the main hall, he heard a sound. Foot-steps. The guard? Had he become suspicious?

Was he coming this way?

Paige moved even faster then stopped in front of his old office. He saw the anxiety written in the dark pools of her eyes.

He yanked his old key from his pocket. The key to his office door had been with him for two years. He didn't even know why he hadn't thrown it away. Had he really ever believed he'd come back?

Maybe he'd lied to himself more than he knew.

The footsteps approached the end of the corridor when it turned into the one where they stood. Another second and someone, possibly the security officer, would turn the corner. He struggled with the key, the lock refusing to budge.

Then the lock clicked, quiet in the eerie gloom of the late-night corridor.

Paige rushed forward into the pitch-black of the office. Kieran spun to shut the door in the nick of time. It would automatically relock. If the officer was coming to check things out, they'd have seconds.

"Hurry," Paige whispered. "Please."

He reached for the switch by feel. The overhead office light sprang on, stung his eyes. He went immediately to the storage cabinet against the rear wall behind the desk. The shelves jangled as he unlocked the cabinet with the same key that worked the office door. Boxes of office supplies loaded the shelves.

The fragile bud of hope inside him died.

But he turned, tore open the desk drawers, then the filing cabinet.

"No, it was here. In the storage cabinet." Paige's voice came raw, cutting through his own despair.

He made himself say it. Made himself accept the fact. "If it was here, it's gone now."

"It can't be," Paige whispered. "I saw it. It was here."

The pain in her eyes slayed him when he turned and met her gaze. "It's going to be okay, Paige." But it wasn't. He was lying, and she knew it. "I have to get the computer booted up." At least no one was banging down the door. Whoever had been coming up the hall, they hadn't been coming to see who was with Paige.

That didn't mean they had all the time in the world, though. He had to not think about what it could mean now that the hope he'd carried of finding the serum was taken. He could still go after the traitor in PAX. He could take his revenge for what they'd done to him and to Paige.

The computer screen blinked on. He could feel the tension in Paige as she knelt beside him. "You're going to have to use your password," he said. "Mine won't work."

She leaned across him and logged into the covert operations network. "What do you want me to search on?" she asked.

"I'll do it." He inputted the names of several key chemicals in the development of the serums. Anyone trying to recreate the activation serum would need them, and no one would have been looking. No one would have been suspicious.

Talia's name came up time and again in the orders. He printed the pages.

He went to the file room screen and again searched on the foundation research that would be kept there from other studies that had led up to the ectoplasmic project.

"Talia," Paige breathed. "What now?"

"Now we get out of here." Kieran pushed the print button. The printer spit out the file records. "Then we make sure Talia pays."

They reached the door. Paige could feel Kieran's heat and strength as he leaned against it, listening. She was more scared than ever. The containment serum was gone. No matter what happened now, Kieran thought he was going to die.

She hurt, inside and out, from all the danger they'd

been through, but nothing hurt more than her heart at the thought of Kieran not making it. A frown marred his features for a moment then he grabbed her hand. His body against hers felt like one solid muscle and she couldn't imagine him dying.

"Come on," he whispered.

The office door clicked quietly open and shut behind them. They raced to the end of the corridor then Kieran stopped, clearly hearing or sensing something she couldn't.

The security lobby was eerily silent to her ears. She held her breath, something prickling the back of her neck. She took a tentative step, leaning forward to see the security booth.

A gasp strangled in her throat. Something red splattered the glass of the booth.

Oh, God.

She felt Kieran's hand tighten on hers. Her pulse throbbed in her ears. Nausea rose and she fought it back, forced her feet to move, driven by the urgent instinct to figure out what was going on, to help if she could. She tore free from Kieran's hand.

Inside the security booth, monitors tipped at crazy angles and the security officer lay on his back, throat opened in a jagged slash. Whatever had happened to him, he was beyond help. She stumbled backward in horror into Kieran's hard chest.

"The elevator," she choked out, and started to race

for it, but Kieran grabbed her back, his face intense, grim. Listening.

The light above the elevator blinked on, indicating the doors were about to open. A muted sound broke the metallic air. Scratching, clawing.

Snarling.

Her heart thudded. Kieran pulled her away, his hold desperate and determined. "Run," he whispered.

The hall felt as if it swerved beneath her feet as she rushed down its endless length. They were going deeper into PAX instead of escaping it—but whatever was behind those elevator doors was even more terrifying. They tore down the corridor, around a corner.

Kieran stopped suddenly and she almost tripped. He pulled her up, held her close. She had to resist the panicked urge to climb up his lean, rock-hard body. They stood there, breathing, listening.

There was a clattering sound from the security lobby. The horror of the security officer's death flashed over and over in her head, like a movie that wouldn't stop playing.

The sound was coming this way.

They were in the short hallway that led to his lab. He dragged the key back out of his pocket. "In here." He pushed Paige down the hall, stuck the key in the door, and they were in.

The dark was thick and smelled of chemicals.

The sound kept coming.

"What is it?" she asked, breaking into shivers. "What's out there?" *And how were they going to escape it?*

In the pitch-black, she couldn't see Kieran. She felt him move away from her and her pulse went into instant overdrive as she snatched his hand. Wherever he was going, she was going.

The light burst on in the lab. Kieran turned back from the switch, and his face was the first thing she saw.

His expression filled her with dread.

And outside the lab door, the sound kept coming.

She turned.

Kieran's lab had been left sealed as it was, not renovated. Closed down and its memory washed clean from PAX, or so they'd told her. No one in the Pentagon had been willing to authorize restarting the project.

The lab gleamed under the fluorescent light. Computers and laboratory equipment laid out in orderly precision. The ramifications of what she was seeing swept over her in a scary wave.

Kieran had been right. Someone in PAX, the traitor, had been working all this time to recreate the serums. But they'd still wanted Kieran—

Paige spun, shaking, to see Kieran flip the inside bolt. There was a bang outside the lab, something thudding against the door. Her pulse gave an answering staccato.

"Is it going to hold?" she breathed.

"It's locked from the inside now."

Her voice came out in a sick, quavering whisper. *"What's out there?"*

She knew the answer before he spoke.

"Werewolves."

"How can that be?" Her throat was so thick with fear, she could barely get the words out. "They need the activation serum. That's why they're after you."

"They have it, somehow. Or they had it. Who knows what happened two years ago before Phil died, but they have it." His gaze rolled back to the lab door. "And they've used it."

The sense of onrushing horror pumped in her blood and nothing in the dread of his eyes was making her feel any better.

"This was a trap, Paige. Maybe the trigger was on your bio-read, not mine. Or maybe they were just watching. They were ready for us. We thought getting into PAX was going to be the trick." A bitter sound came from his throat. "It's getting out that's going to be the problem."

No one would be here at this hour, no one but security, and they'd taken care of the officer at the central station already. But why wasn't more security coming? The security cameras on the main floor of PAX were connected to other top-level security stations throughout the building.

"But who could do this? Who could take over PAX this way?" Who would have had access to Kieran's sealed lab? Talia couldn't have that kind of power.

Whatever creatures had been out there, they'd gone frighteningly silent. Her pulse thumped, the silence worse than the sounds.

Kieran moved across the lab, stealthy, competent, terrifyingly determined. Then she heard what he must already have sensed. A sound broke through the taut air, emanating from the lab storage closet.

Paige followed him, panic rising again in her already too-full throat.

Kieran took his gun into his fist, cocked it, and in one flashing movement yanked open the storage closet door.

"No." Paige reached for him, fearing another trap, then a cry lodged in her throat.

Talia Regan lay on the closet floor, tied and bleeding.

Talia had a black eye and a swollen cheekbone. Her temple bled from a jagged cut.

She sat propped against the wall of the lab, her eyes huge and dark, her normally perfect auburn hair tangled in limp strands on her cheeks.

"I found the money in the account," she whispered, her voice trembling. "I started asking questions, because I knew the source was a foreign agency, the one we'd thought Phil and Kieran were working with to sell the serums. I went to David Rodale, and then the next thing I knew, his whole family was dead and so was he."

She looked from Paige to Kieran, her liquid eyes shimmering. "I was so scared. I didn't say anything to anyone else for a long time. I was scared of ending up…like them." She shivered. "I knew it had something to do with the explosion, with what Phil and Kieran—" She broke off, shook her head. "I knew there was someone else involved, someone in PAX, because I started noticing the files and chemicals being checked out in my name. I was afraid to do anything—afraid if I told another member of the task force, they'd end up dead, too. I started thinking Kieran had been framed. They told me there had been a reactant found in the lab when they did the forensics—a reactive agent that had caused the explosion. I realized anyone could have mislabeled the chemicals. Anyone with the power to get into this lab. They thought Kieran had done it, that he'd intended to kill Phil and been caught in the explosion himself. But I knew that whoever had checked out those files and chemicals in my name, whoever had placed that money in that account, had to have been the one."

Acids with acids, bases with bases. The simplest of science manipulated to create the greatest of horrors. Paige's stomach turned.

Talia looked at Paige again, her eyes pleading and desperate. "I wanted you to find Kieran, but I couldn't tell you why. I knew I needed help, and I was so afraid of putting anyone in danger. I thought Shay was suspicious of the findings after the explosion—I know he wanted Kieran back desperately, too. But after what happened to David— I knew Kieran had to be in danger already. Someone had already tried to kill him. I never wanted you to be in danger, too, Paige." Tears filled in her eyes.

A lump of regret grew in Paige's chest. "I wish you'd told me."

"I didn't want you to die." Tears streaked Talia's cheeks now. She reached up to wipe them away, the skin where her wrists had been tied raw. "I just wanted to find Kieran and I knew the only way was through you. I'm so sorry."

"Don't be," Paige whispered thickly, then took a breath, steadied her emotions. "What about Brian? How did you get his cell phone?"

"He called me and set up a meeting. When I got there, he was dead—ripped apart, as if by an animal. I took his phone—and Kieran called." She blinked back more tears. "But you hung up before I could tell you anything."

"Someone was after us," Paige explained. "We had to run. And then— Then we didn't know who we could trust. We'd found out about the money in the account, too. And we found the files and the chemical orders. We thought you were involved."

"That's how he made it look."

"Who?" Kieran's granite hard jaw seethed tension. *"Who is behind this?"*

Talia squeezed her eyes shut for an aching beat. "I found a log book. I found the record of the experiments. He's been experimenting for two years." She lifted her lashes, her gaze shining, haunted. "Phil had given him a sample of the activation serum. He thought there was more, thought he had an entire case of the serum, and he was going to double-cross Phil—plant the evidence on Phil and on Kieran and blow up the lab. That way, all the money would be his. But Phil double-crossed him, too. Phil must have been suspicious because the vials were empty, except for one. He used it before he realized that was all he had. He used it on himself and on a sampling of men he'd recruited from the terrorist group. He wanted to know if it would work, and as long as he kept experimenting, dragging it out, giving them little bits of information at a time, they kept paying him."

"Who is he?" Kieran demanded. He knelt by Talia. "Where did you find this log book?"

"In my father's office!" she breathed, and tears spilled fresh down her face.

Shock gripped Paige. She saw Kieran's face drain, and knew hers must look the same. *Vinn.* Vinn, who would have had the power to manipulate all this evidence. Vinn, who would have had the power to trip the security any time he needed. Vinn, who had been in the apartment that morning and planted the serum.

And they were trapped in PAX with his band of men empowered now with the serum. Vinn had to be here, too. Somewhere. And he was activated.

"Brian told me he'd known all along," Talia said. "He ran away. He was scared for his life. But his conscience got to him and he told me before we met that he'd seen Vinn plant the documents at Phil's house, the ones that implicated Kieran in the plot. I knew then that there was no doubt. It was my father." A sob choked her words. "Brian was going to come with me tonight, to break into the office, but when I went to meet him, he was dead. I went to my father's office tonight, alone. I had stolen his key. I found the log book and then—"

"He found you," Paige breathed.

"It was terrible," Talia went on softly. "He was enraged. He admitted he'd put the money in an account in my name, used my name to order files and chemicals." Her gaze tore to Kieran. "He'd sacrifice anyone, even his own daughter, for his greed. He thought if he used my name, he'd get away with it. He was sure I wouldn't turn him in, even if I noticed. And if I tried—"

She would be destroyed, just like Kieran had been.

"He doesn't have any more of the activation serum," Talia said, and she grasped Kieran's arm suddenly. "He's determined to get it, though. He knows it works and he wants more. He wants to sell it. And he's desperate. His plot is crumbling around him. He'll do anything now."

"Where is he?" Kieran asked her, his voice deadly and so detached. Paige could see the dark resolution in his eyes. He wanted to confront Vinn.

"I woke up here," Talia told them. "I don't know where he is."

"We know where his men are," Paige said. "They're here, inside PAX. We broke in to find the evidence—against you, we thought." She felt dizzy still at the bizarre contrast of what they'd believed and what they now knew was true. "We couldn't get out. The security guard in the lobby is dead. His men were coming out of the elevator. They'd already shifted."

The activation serum in the hands of someone evil was a horrific reality.

"Why hasn't more security come?" Paige asked.

"He switched off the system," Talia said. "He has to have switched off the system to this floor."

Paige's pulse thumped. No help would be coming. They were on their own.

"What about the containment serum?" Kieran asked abruptly.

Talia reached into her pocket. "I found it in his office before he caught me. He doesn't know I have it." A vial rolled out of her palm and onto the floor.

Paige's gaze wheeled to Kieran.

There was a distant sound, a bang, then a scratching noise from somewhere above. Kieran's face rose.

His stark whisper cut the dread. "They're going to come in through the air ducts."

Chapter 14

He took the vial of precious serum. It was only partially depleted. Vinn would have used it. But the men he'd recruited— There wouldn't be any containment serum left if they'd used it, too.

Kieran swung on Talia again. "Did you get a chance to read much of the log? Do you know how they were activated?"

He'd been contaminated in the worst way, through the explosion. The serum's chemicals had been burned into his cells. It wasn't the way the activation had been intended to work. And it was why he'd always questioned whether or not the containment serum would even function properly on him, even if he could have created it in time.

"Injection," Talia said.

Paige's wide, anxious eyes locked with his. "What does that mean?" He didn't answer right away, and she left Talia, leaped to her feet and came over to him at the lab counter. "What difference does it make?"

"The activation won't be as strong as it was for me, in the explosion," he told her, steeling himself for what he knew now he had to do.

The thump and scratch above came again. They were working their way through the ducts. They didn't have much time.

He had to take the risk, for her and for PAX. He turned toward the lab cabinet, rifled through the chemicals for a reactive agent that would interact with the serum's makeup. He steadied his mind as he took down a reactant and prayed his plan would work. He placed it on the lab counter. His hands were shaking.

It could make a deadly combination. He looked up at Paige. Behind her, Talia had risen, her eyes wide, her stride stumbling.

"The containment serum was intended to give the subject complete control of the transformation," he explained. "But if the activation was injected, there could be a way to apply the containment so that it *could*—" he emphasized the word *could* because, hell, he didn't know and all he could do now was try based on his own years of conjecture and experimentation with the serum "—deactivate the change completely—if it's applied in a more powerful, more devastating way."

To deactivate by injection would take the entire vial. And there were too many of them, and no way to inject them anyway.

Paige had come near him, so near he could smell her sweet, fresh scent, filling him with a yearning to tangle his hands in her hair one last time and claim her with a blinding kiss. Claim the life and hope she offered.

There was another thump from above again.

Paige jumped at the sound. "We have to get out of here."

"Vinn's out there," Kieran reminded her. His heart pounded and dread streamed through his blood. "And they're up there." Divide and conquer, that's what they had to do. The vial of valuable serum, serum that could save his life felt heavy and cold in his fist. "We have to deactivate them."

"How?" The question tore out of her.

"They're going to come down through those vents in a few minutes. And I'm going to blow this serum sky high."

Horror filled Paige's gaze. "But you need the serum to survive!"

"We need to survive the next five minutes, too," he pointed out. He was scaring her, badly, almost as much as the creatures coming ever closer in those air ducts above them. But he had no choice. *They* had no choice. "The explosion should fire off the alarms. Even if Vinn's manipulated the security cameras from this floor, the alarms will bring help." And God, they needed help.

"But what about you?"

"I don't think it will deactivate me. They were injected, I wasn't. It could be *exactly* what I need. It could save me, Paige."

He was telling her a fairy tale. He was telling her what she wanted to hear. Or maybe it was what he wanted to hear, too. There was nothing tested, nothing known for certain, about this serum. But if the containment serum was burned into his cellular structure the same way the activation serum had been…

She grabbed hold of his arms. "Don't lie to me!"

One tortured beat. Two.

"Vinn's waiting out there, Paige. He's sending them in to flush us out. This is our only chance. We neutralize them then we deal with Vinn."

Silence. Then the thumping from above. Louder. Closer.

"We?" she breathed softly.

He reached for the waistband of his jeans where he'd jammed the gun. He pushed it into Paige's hand.

"The explosion's going to blow that door." He looked at her with fear pumping his heart hard against the wall of his chest. He didn't want her out there, alone, with Vinn, and all he could do was pray to God that he would be with her in here, that this application of the containment serum wouldn't kill him. But if he wasn't, she would have the gun. She would have a chance. "The chemicals in the containment serum won't hurt you, but the explosion could—when I throw the reactant, I want you down. And as soon as that door blows, run. I'll be right behind you." He hoped.

She stood there, shaking, and yet staring at him with those damnably resolute eyes of hers. "I won't leave you," she said, her voice low but hot. "Not now. Not ever." She swallowed hard and she reached a suddenly steady hand to his face. Her touch seared his heart. He saw her draw a breath, straighten her shoulders, and her eyes shone with all the strength inside her. "I love you. And we're going to do this together."

His heart felt like it was in a million pieces and whole all at the same time. And then there was no more time.

The cover to the air duct struck the floor.

A dark, lean blur dropped from the ceiling, landing on all fours. Talia screamed as another one dropped.

A third shapeshifter growled in the opening, hesitating, sniffing at the scene below. Then it dropped, too. Together, they spread out, circling in a band toward where Talia, Kieran and Paige stood.

Three, there were three. And he prayed that was all. Nothing more dropped from the ducts.

The one closest raised its tail, put its ears forward, lifted its lips in a fearsome snarl. The fur along its back hackled.

Kieran grabbed the vial of containment serum. The lead wolf reared its head back suddenly and let loose a piercing howl. The others barked in unison, the harmony a deadly threat and no doubt a communication to Vinn.

Then they lowered their heads and moved in for the kill. Kieran felt his own body itching, burning, prickling to change, and he resisted with agonizing will. Not yet. Not now.

"Down!" Kieran shouted. Paige and Talia dove as he heaved the vial of containment serum. It shattered and he crashed the reactant across the room after it.

He lifted his hands, shielding his face and praying he could withstand the force that he knew would burn those chemicals straight through his cells in the first seconds of the blast. The world boomed and he slammed backward, knocking against the lab counter, crashing onto the floor.

Inside his body, he felt the immediate hum and

crackle of the chemical reaction. Stinging, cramps, fever, only this time it wasn't as if it were exploding out of his skin but rather into it, spinning inside himself. Everything went black.

He was going to die, and the long-damaged part of him had waited for this moment, waited for it all to end. But through the pain, he saw Paige's face lit with life, remembered her warm lips on his mouth, her hope on his heart.

I love you.

Paige was out there. His eyes flashed open to a universe of spitting flame and shattering light. Alarms shrilled from somewhere outside the lab.

I won't leave you. Not ever.

But she was gone. He couldn't see Paige.

He rammed to his feet, the laboratory a spooky swamp of smoke and licking flames and shattered glass from the beakers on the shelves. Then he saw her and his heart wrenched in both pride and fear. The precious woman he'd thought *he* needed to protect was standing in the middle of it all, aiming the gun at the men rising from the floor toward her and Talia, ready to save *his* life.

The men—men now, not wolves—rose and lunged toward her. She didn't hesitate. She fired off three shots, and Vinn's men blew backward one after another. But before relief could hit, beyond where Paige stood Kieran spied a fourth figure emerge through the cloud of fire from the direction of the lab door.

The lab door that must have been blown as he'd predicted.

His throat burned raw and he couldn't make his voice work. He staggered, dizzy from the chemical reaction inside his body.

For the first time, Kieran saw the change outside himself. Saw Vinn's violent eyes light with a glow from within, but it wasn't the change he'd expected. He didn't see proportions shifting, shoulders sliding into his torso. It was a more subtle change, controlled. Vinn remained on two legs. His body wasn't that of a wolf but of a wolf-man. Hair prickled from his face and his teeth elongated. His stature seemed to swell and his entire body loomed larger than life. The containment serum worked! It really worked. And as soon as that hope bloomed in Kieran's chest, bleak despair raged back in.

"Paige!" he rasped, struggling to reach her in time.

Shift! He had to shift!

Kieran knew an awesome power ripping through his own body. Only it wasn't agonizing now. It was warm, fast, easy, and he felt an amazing control, an incredible sense of direction and he welcomed the change, welcomed the fierce strength. His senses didn't shatter. He didn't lose himself.

It was as if he'd found himself instead. Found an incredible force that was his to command.

And even as Vinn arced through the air toward Paige, he leaped.

* * *

Paige hit the floor of the lab with a jarring thud as Vinn struck her. Her heart jumped into her throat, blood pounded through her body. She could feel his thick hands on her shoulders, whipping her around. Her head thunked back on the floor and she saw black for a sickening beat. Then his body disappeared, air and heat pushing past her.

Through blurred eyes, she saw Kieran—not a wolf and yet with the shocking power of one—blow Vinn back against the wall. There was a cracking thud as Vinn's body slammed, then he was on his feet again, rebounding with unbelievable energy. Kieran snarled and dove at him again, and the two men grappled together onto the floor.

The lab still flickered in the spit of dying chemicals, flames eating across the floor toward the two men. Talia scrambled back beside Paige, her face filled with shadows and horror. Paige tried to rise, her head dizzying. She felt shards of glass littering the floor everywhere, cutting into her body.

The gun! Where was the gun?

She couldn't see it, and she couldn't watch this fight and not do something. She forced herself to her feet, staggered to the lab counter, choking on the smoke, stumbling around curling puddles of liquid fire. She grabbed the first thing she saw that looked like it could be a weapon.

The two men were separated now, snarling, circling each other. Two breathtaking bestial powers unleashed. The alarms stopped shrilling but the spitting fire and angry gasps filled the silence.

"You should have come over to my side," Vinn growled at Kieran, his face contorted in rage and violent energy. "You could have been rich. You could have had everything."

"I have a soul," Kieran hissed. "Unlike you."

"I had my men tracking you," Vinn carried on, and he danced backward as Kieran took aim at him with his powerful arm. "The pilot was one of mine. I suppose you know that by now. Fools that they were they lost you. Fools that you were, you ran, and kept running. I might have let you live, you know. I have a soft spot for you and Paige."

"Like the soft spot you have for your own daughter?" Kieran asked harshly.

Vinn shrugged in cruel nonchalance, baring his teeth. "She would have betrayed me."

"Like you betrayed PAX?"

"It's not too late!" Vinn shouted.

His back was to Paige now. She inched closer with the heavy centrifugal pump she'd torn from its mount on the lab counter.

"You hear those alarms?" Kieran shouted. "It's over, Vinn. It's really over."

"Not yet," Vinn hissed, and without making a single move to show he knew Paige was there, he flung back a massive arm and struck her full in the face. The pump flew and Paige hit the floor with a smack.

Her world was only sound and sensation for a brutal beat. She opened her eyes to see Kieran's snarling lunge and then the two men grappled again until with a mighty kick, Kieran flung Vinn backward. Kieran loomed in the shattering light of the lab, huge. The other man scrambled backward, struck against her leg.

She couldn't move, could barely breathe the choking air, her head one dizzying staccato of pain, but she felt the sudden embrace of Vinn's cruel arms as he twisted around and dragged her up, onto her stumbling feet. Something jagged scraped her neck, and Kieran knelt, lifted something heavy and dark, and she knew where the gun was now. He'd found it.

"I'll slice her throat," Vinn gasped. Paige felt the shard of broken glass dig into her neck. "I've got a helicopter on the roof. Come with me. Give me the secrets of the serums—or she dies right here, right now."

Agony blazed from Kieran's hollow eyes as he straightened the arm holding the gun. "There's no way I'll ever give you the serum formulas, Vinn."

"Then you have a decision to make, son. And you don't have much time. I might as well be dead if I can't get out of here with the serums. They're going to kill me, you know."

Paige saw the flinch in Kieran's hollowed eyes at the reference to him as a son. Vinn had been like his father. Too much so. He'd been betrayed by both of his fathers.

"Make your decision," Vinn growled, and she felt his heat, felt the shard of glass biting into her neck. Did he want to die? The thought burst into her head and she felt her heart breaking for the man he might have been if he hadn't let his greed destroy the good she knew had been in his heart once.

"But I'm not going to be ruined alone. I'll kill her." Vinn's voice came to her ear in a sick taunt, and the pity she wanted to feel for him died. Then all she knew was pain as the shard cut deeper.

Then a deafening explosion rang out. The world seemed to spin away, and all she could see was the agony in Kieran's eyes. All she could feel was Vinn's arms falling away from her. She wheeled, dizzy, to find Vinn on the floor, a neat hole in his forehead.

Then she felt arms swoop around her, safe, warm, wonderful arms, pulling her through the doorway, out of the smoke and fire and madness.

"Are you all right?" Kieran whispered as he set her down outside the lab, his hands brushing at her hair, shaking as they held her face. And even as he held her, she could see him changing, morphing, sliding back into his human self. But before he did, she touched him, felt the strangeness of his face, Kieran but not Kieran as it changed.

Then he was Kieran again, complete and whole. Free of the overpowering control of his wolf side. In control, able to shift without losing himself—and shift back.

"I'm perfect," she whispered. And she was, because Kieran was holding her. Her head reeled and her body ached but none of it mattered.

"You're bleeding!" His anxious hands tightened on her.

"I'm alive," she whispered. "And so are you. And you're okay." She leaned into those dear hands that held her face and he pulled her close, claimed her in a blistering kiss that said everything she needed to know.

But then he drew back enough to breathe against her lips, "I love you, Paige. And you were right, about everything. I pushed you away. I wanted to see if you'd go. And dammit, you just wouldn't. And now there's no time but I just wanted you to know—"

Heart in her throat, she choked out, "There's time. Say it again."

"I love you. You know I love you."

She didn't know if she wanted to laugh or cry. "I know. But it's good to hear." And then she was sobbing and he was kissing every tear.

"But you know how messed up my life is now,"

he said shakily when he drew away. "*I'm* messed up. We got out of this alive, but it's not over. And it's not going to be over for me, and you have to know that. This isn't a cure, and I don't want you to think that. I'm alive, and maybe the containment serum worked. We don't know how well, won't know how well for a while. There'll have to be tests, and God, I don't know if I'm even going to be a free man. I don't want your pity—"

"I don't feel sorry for you," she burst out. He was worried about what would happen to him now, worried that his life was still a wreck. All she cared about was that he *had* a life. "Stop trying to push me away," she added thickly.

She realized with a shock there were tears in his eyes. "I don't want to push you away, not anymore. I want to do the opposite. I want to ask you to be my wife."

Now she started crying in earnest. "We're already married," she pointed out, her voice breaking.

He held her, cradling her in his arms. "I want to buy you a minivan—"

"I don't want a minivan," she cried softly and touched his cheek, loved him. "I lied." She laughed, the sound a hitch on a sob. "I don't want an ordinary life. I want an extraordinary one—with you."

He kept holding her, and she never wanted him to stop. Then she saw the shadows shift, lifted her gaze to see over Kieran's shoulder, down the hall. PAX agents rushed toward them. There were going to be a lot of questions. And finally, he had answers.

Epilogue

It was just an ordinary brownstone on an ordinary Washington, D.C., street. The autumn air was crisp with the nip of turning weather, and oaks dripped golden leaves on the shadowed street. Kieran turned the lock of the glass-fronted door, and his steady nerves gave a little flip at the glow of joy in his wife's eyes.

She was stubborn, though.

"Aren't you going to carry me over the threshold?" she teased.

"I'll carry you anywhere, Mrs. Holt," he growled and easily swung her into his arms. He deposited her gently on the hardwood floor of the very-empty living room. Wide windows looked out onto the wooded back.

She lifted her face, closed her eyes, and took a long, long breath, then released it. He felt a resonating release inside his heart. The months that had gone by since that fateful night at PAX had been one long exhale.

"Home," Paige breathed, opening her beautiful eyes to him. "Finally."

It had taken three months to get through the intensive investigation following Vinn Regan's death and the discovery of the secret experiments in the sealed lab. A new PAX chief had been named, and new oversight procedures had been put in place to prevent any PAX chief in the future, or any agent in PAX at all, from having the power alone to carry out such a plot again. The agency had experienced its darkest hour, and through it, had found the core of determination to continue on its mission to achieve a better world. *Peace through PAX.*

Kieran had withstood the probing analysis of the explosion two years ago and his subsequent flight to Callula Island, and in light of Vinn's stunning betrayal and the evidence found in the lab and in the PAX chief's home, Kieran had been found innocent of all charges. He'd borne the medical examinations that had finally determined him to be fit for continued duty with his ectoplasmic powers under full control—and in fact, he was more valuable to PAX than ever with his knowledge and experience. The physical and psychological exams had proven he was healthy. The containment serum had worked. The government had backed a new round of testing and development on alternative species transfers, and Kieran had been offered the assignment.

During the downtime during the months of unaccustomed leave from work, he'd endured what he reminded Paige often had to be the most grueling house hunt in the history of Washington, D.C. He hadn't really been complaining. He'd loved every minute trailing around the city with his amazing wife who'd proven he didn't have to save the day alone. And he never wanted to try again.

They'd renewed their vows just two weeks ago, following the official end of the investigation. It had been the happiest day of his life. Then the next one had been happy, too. And the one after that.

There were still hard days amidst the happiness. He still grieved the PAX chief he'd once so admired. And Talia had left PAX despite Kieran and Paige's encouragement to stay on as had been their decision. But Talia's resolve had remained firm, and they'd accepted that she had to deal with the betrayal and loss in her own way.

Dub was back in Savannah. Fishing, along with his other mysterious activities. He'd helped Kieran get in touch with Harry, and together they were planning to make sure the cabin at Buck's Run was rebuilt. Harry, immersed in his studies in South America, hadn't seemed overly concerned, but Kieran took full responsibility for the destruction. And there was maybe a little part of him that saw his children some day playing where he and Annelie had played in the fresh start that would be that new cabin.

He liked that picture, that fresh start.

"We'll put the Christmas tree right there," Paige whispered, gazing over his shoulder at the perfect spot just between the windows. She grabbed Kieran's arm and dragged him across their newly-purchased house. "And the dining room table here." She pulled him into the kitchen. "I'll have to strip all that wallpaper, of course." She gazed around, pinched her pretty brows. "And paint. Yellow, I think. We should do it before the furniture is delivered, don't you think?"

"No ladders," Kieran said automatically. "No paint fumes." He reached out and put his hand on the bloom of her pregnant stomach. "Not for our baby."

Paige pursed her lips in a little frown then laughed and he knew she'd been teasing. "Just checking to see if your protection meter is still working. You win this one. For the baby."

It was the baby they'd made on their treacherous trek back to PAX, and somehow it felt just right that in those bleak hours, hope had stomped right in and planted its rebellious flag.

Kieran leaned in to lay a soft kiss on her sweet lips. "I'm definitely the big winner," he growled. He had his life, his work, his home, and his wife. And the future he'd never believed possible had never seemed more real.

Tears brimmed in Paige's eyes. "Me, too," she whispered. "*We're* the winners."

* * * * *

HARLEQUIN®
Next™